AF267633

Fighting for the King

B. Heather Mantler

Lit-N-Laughter

ISBN:1927507200
ISBN-13:9781927507209
Library and Archives Canada Cataloguing in Publication

Mantler, B. Heather, 1987-, author
 Fighting for the king / B. Heather Mantler.

ISBN 978-1-927507-20-9 (paperback)
 I. Title.

PS8626.A676F53 2015 C813'.6 C2015-905768-X

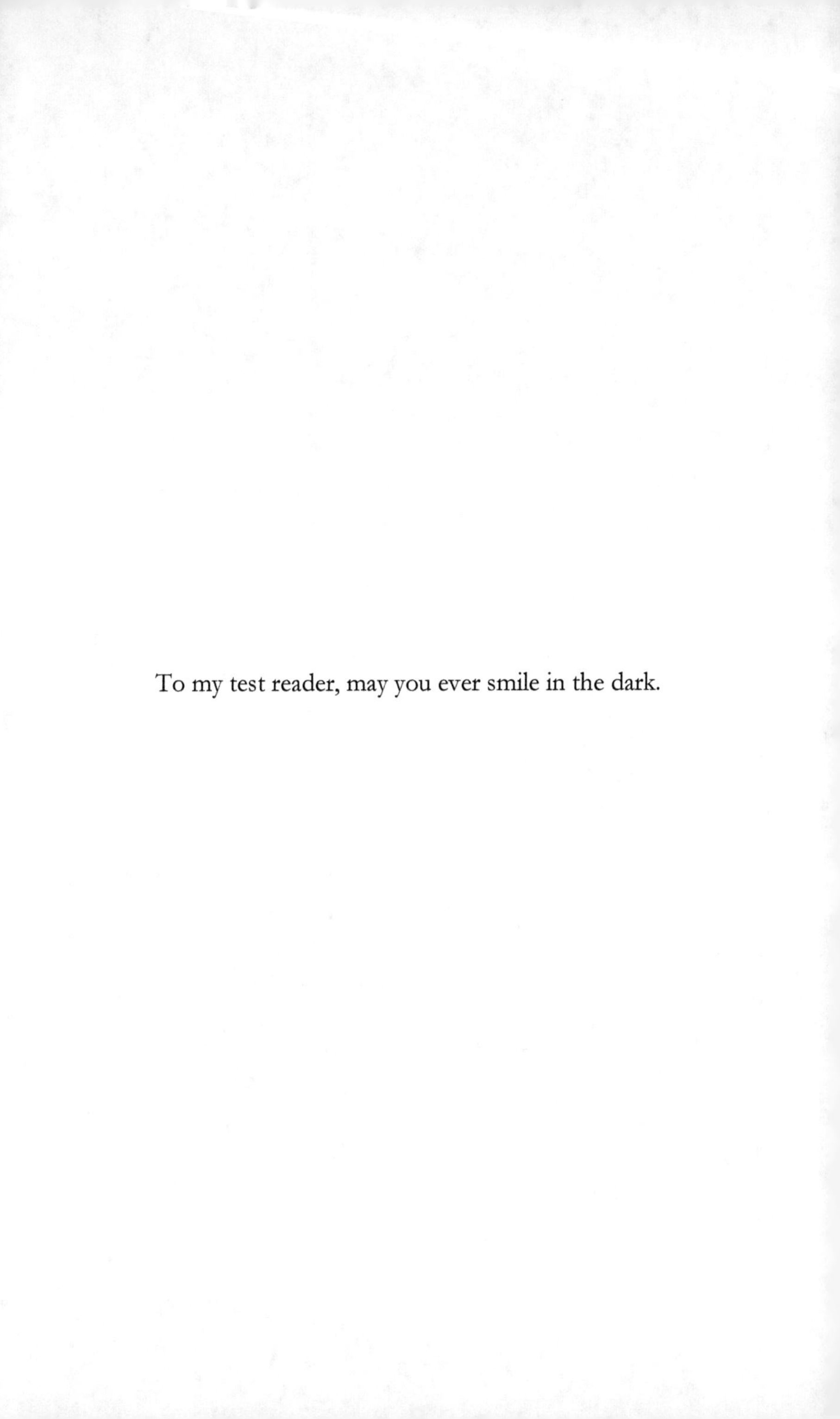

To my test reader, may you ever smile in the dark.

A STORY FOR THE CHILD KING

Waldemar, the child king of Proster, wandered down the row of shelves in the library as he looked for a book to have his mother, Arabella, read a bedtime story. She had finished the last one yesterday, so he needed to find a new book. The last book had been suggested by Weldon, the Duke, and had some strong lessons about being a king. Waldemar did not care for those kinds of stories, and he heard a lifetime's worth of them already.

"Hurry up, Waldemar," Arabella called from the hallway.

Waldemar finally found the section where he had seen the adventure stories. He could not reach the ones on the higher shelves, but there were some on a shelf he could reach. After studying the selection a moment, Waldemar took Adventures for a Future King by Thomas Merritt off the shelf and headed for the door. His mother was waiting in the hallway with her hands on her hips and a stern look on her face.

"You should have been in bed fifteen minutes ago,"

Arabella said.

"I found a book," Waldemar held it up for inspection. Arabella took it and looked over the cover.

"Fine," Arabella said, "Get ready for bed and I will be up in a moment to read it to you."

"Thank you, Mother," Waldemar said before taking off down the hallway. He ran the whole way to his room, where Eldon was preparing what was necessary for Waldemar to be ready for bed.

"Mother is coming," Waldemar said stepping up on the stool and putting his arms out.

"Yes, Sire," Eldon said. Eldon pulled Waldemar's shirt over his head and off. While he was folding that, Waldemar took off his pants. Eldon caught them before they hit the floor. Eldon took the nightshirt off the bed and tugged it down over Waldemar's head.

Waldemar stepped off the stool, and Eldon pulled back the covers so Waldemar could climb into bed. Then he removed the clothing. He let Arabella into the room as he left. She closed the door before sitting down in the chair beside the bed.

"I will only read a short amount," Arabella said, "You are already late getting to bed, and you need to be up early tomorrow morning."

"Yes, Mother," Waldemar settled against his pillow and waited for her to start.

"Adventures of a Future King by Thomas Merritt," Arabella read the cover before opening it and turning to the first page of the story, "Once upon a time in a kingdom south of any place you could go, a boy was going along a forest path.

He had said, "I am going out for a walk." His mother merely handed James a sandwich and reminded him to be back in time for supper. That had been couple of hours ago. He was now certain that suppertime would come and go without his return. No more hoeing, or raking, or digging he thought. No more farming of any type was his plan and leaving his mother and step-father behind was required to reach that end.

The trees were getting larger, the bushes were now sparse and the path more shaded. Then he came upon the sign post where the trail diverged and he stood for a few minutes deciding upon his destination. Since he was literate he knew that right was Greeneves and to the left was the market town where his step-father bought and sold his produce.

His step-father claimed that was where the better deals were. James knew the man lied about it, but having never been the Greeneves he did not know why. Well, this would be James's chance to see Greeneves, if he wanted to see it. James frowned at the hesitation.

The thought of leaving his mother behind nagged slightly at his heels but James was adamant about not farming anymore and so he had to find another way to earn his keep as his step-father was fond of telling him. So there was nothing to do but press onward. He started towards Greeneves.

Now James had been wandering along this path for some time and had seen nothing of interest. He wondered if he had picked the wrong path, but really did not feel like going back to try the other one. Still he had met no travelers, even animals were apparently spars. James stopped in the middle of the path and sat down to rest a moment. He had been walking for the morning and he was ready for lunch. However, he did not take the sandwich into his hand nor eat it, because at that moment a man stepped out of the darkness created by the trees. His presence had gone undetected by James until that moment and not noticing the man upset James' sense of security.

"Ah, here you are," the man was dressed in green of varying shades, except for his boots which were black, "I have been waiting

for you."

"How can you be expecting me?" James asked, "I did not know I was coming this direction until I arrived."

"Do you think it is chance you happened to be at this spot at this moment?" the man asked.

"Yes," James answered, "No one could have manipulated the events which placed me here."

"Ah, but there you would be wrong," the man said, "You have been destined to be here since before you were born."

"And why would that be?" James asked.

"You are currently in search of an adventure, are you not?" the man asked.

"Yes," James answered.

"Then I am going to provide you with one," the man said.

"And you are?" James asked.

"Kendrick," the man answered.

"Where are we going?" James asked.

"Greeneves for now," Kendrick answered.

James sat quietly for a moment before getting to his feet. "Lead on," James said. Kendrick nodded before starting along the path. James let the strange man in green get five steps ahead of him before following him. The man did not look back, he just assumed James would follow where he led. James saw no reason not to go with this man to Greeneves, as it was his destination at the moment anyway.

They did not speak as they walked and James was always five steps behind Kendrick. The path was clear as was the sky above the branches. They did not stop to rest, or eat, and James wondered if the man ahead of him was something other than human. He had never met someone who did not need to stop to catch his breath. James' own stomach complained about all the energy he expended without eating, but he could hardly stop now.

The last rays of sunlight shone down on Greeneves by the time they arrived. Greeneves was a village rather than a town. The main street was its longest and widest path and still barely wide enough for a wagon. At one end of the path was a large house with the royal flag hanging down the front, while the other end was the gate into the village. Half way between the two points was the second largest building in the place, which had a sign hanging above the door announced it to be the Trotting Stallion. The establishment was the destination of Kendrick, the strange man in green. James followed him inside as there did not appear to be any other option.

Inside the tavern was a large common room, which was filled with drunks and would be drunks. Kendrick did look about the room, not that James could see an empty chair as it seemed every man in the village was there having a drink. Aside from their drinks, the men were focused on a man beside the fireplace who was playing a fiddle with a happy precision matched by no one James had ever heard. James found himself drawn into the music. The fiddler looked up at him and their eyes met. There was sense of familiarly, but James did not know why. The fiddler broke the eye contact to concentrate on his playing.

Kendrick spoke with the man behind the counter for a brief moment before heading toward a door off the common room. James followed Kendrick and found himself in a private dining room with a long, wooden table flanked by benches, a fire place at one end, and ten other diners. There were two empty spaces at the end opposite from the fire. Kendrick sat down in one chair, leaving James no other choice but to sit down in the other. Those seated were eating and paying no attention to the new comers. James wondered whether he and Kendrick would be served or whether he should take out the food his mother packed him for lunch. The answer arrived when the door opened and the man who had been behind the counter brought in two plates. A plate was placed in front of James and Kendrick before the man withdrew from the room.

James did not bother with any social niceties which he might have otherwise observed. He immediately fell to his meal. As a growing boy, he needed all the nourishment he could acquire in any circumstance. The bread, meat, and cider smelled so good and tasted *even better. They, however, did not last as long as James had hoped and he quickly found himself with an empty plate to go with his half empty stomach.*

As the rest of the men finished their food, they placed their plates in a pile in the middle of the table and waited impatiently for everyone else to do the same. The group turned towards Kendrick. James reluctantly passed his plate down to be added to the pile and sat back.

Although his walking speed was fast, Kendrick was the slowest eater. James was sure snails ate at a faster pace. The rest of the men got restless in their impatience. Wet stones and weapons came out as if it honing them were a normal pastime among this group.

The only man who did not bother with any of that was the man across the table from Kendrick. His outfit was similar to Kendrick. It was various shades of green and included cloak, boots, vest, shirt as well as various pockets for weapons. His dark hair was pushed back from his face to fall to his shoulders. There was a scar on his right cheek where the stubble would not grow. His dark eyes stared at Kendrick as he leaned back with his arms crossed over his chest. An air of authority suggested this man to be the group's leader.

Kendrick was close to finishing when the man from behind the counter in the common room entered. He came and picked up the pile of plates from the table.

"Bring another round of drinks for the men," the man across from Kendrick said.

"Right away," was the response.

"And another plate of supper for the boy," the man said.

"Yes, sir," the man took the plates out the door and closed it behind him.

"I hardly think the second is necessary, Cyrus," Kendrick said, "Supper was plenty for anyone."

"Did you stop for lunch?" Cyrus asked.

"No, but," Kendrick started.

"Enough of your foolish excuses and explain why you called us

all here," Cyrus said, "Unless you have a good reason for our presence, we are leaving."

"I asked for your aide," Kendrick said. He paused, likely for dramatic effect, which was ignored by the others as the man on the other side of Kendrick from James spat on the wet stone. Kendrick took out a map and key and placed them on the table in front of him.

"I received these from a man dying of several arrow wounds," Kendrick said, "He asked me to finish his quest."

"And what was his quest?" Cyrus asked.

"To find the Lost Stone of Uzree," Kendrick answered. The men shook their heads as they muttered "Impossible. Suicide. Idiotic." Cyrus just looked at Kendrick.

"And these should lead us to where the jewel was lost?" Cyrus asked.

"He said they would," Kendrick said, "But there is a deadline. If we do not get the jewel and return with it before the first day of autumn then the royal line loses its power and the kingdom will be passed to the steward to rule."

"The steward should not be allowed anywhere near the throne," the man beside Cyrus said, "He will cause everything to become as evil as he is."

"His plans to destroy the kingdom are well known," Cyrus said, "But what do we get for finishing this quest? You took the map and key from a dying man, who very likely worked for the king and was doing this quest out of loyalty. We have no such motivation for if the steward should become ruler, we can move to another kingdom and find work there."

"If I read the map correctly, the Stone of Uzree is in an orc hoard," Kendrick said, "That means other treasures have found their way there. The rest of the treasure is your reward for finding the stone. Also the king would likely be grateful for the return of the stone and provide a reward for its return."

"But that is uncertain," Cyrus said.

"*There will be a reward,*" Kendrick said, "*I assure you.*"

"*Very well,*" Cyrus said, "*My men and I will do our best to find the jewel. Will you be accompanying us, or going off on your own business?*"

"*I will go along with you only part way,*" Kendrick answered, "*I also ask that you take the boy with you on this quest.*" Kendrick gestured to James. The men gave sour looks at the thought of taking James along with them, but Cyrus stared at James for a minute without speaking. James felt like his soul was being examined.

"*Very well,*" Cyrus said turning back to Kendrick.

The door opened and the drinks were delivered. All the men were given a mug, while James was given another plate of food with a mug of cider. He started into the second helping with as much relish as the first and barely noticed as Cyrus took the key and map from in front of Kendrick.

"*Men,*" Cyrus called, "*Drink to your health and then find space to rest in. We start early tomorrow morning.*"

The men called aye before starting their drinks. They started conversations with those seated nearby them. Cyrus leaned over the table toward Kendrick.

"*If this should be a useless expedition you will pay for it,*" Cyrus told Kendrick in a low tone.

"*All my information is correct,*" Kendrick said.

"*I hope so,*" Cyrus said before leaning back.

James finished his second helping and found himself to be full this time. He leaned back in his chair. The thought of being on a quest was the only thing keeping him awake as the long walk and full stomach were lulling him toward sleep. He was going on a quest to help get back a lost relic and stop the evil in the world from gaining a foothold. It was going to be dangerous, but he was sure he could contribute greatly. All he needed was a chance to show these men what he could do.

James' chin moved closer and closer toward his chest before he could no longer keep his eyes open.

James woke early as his step-father required, but found himself in a dark room not the main room in the farm house where he lived. There were no embers near him for warmth, though he did not feel cold. The blanket he was wrapped in was not the coarse one he was used to, but a smooth one.

As he tried to figure out where he was, James became aware of the snores of others around him. There were at least five different varieties. A body was at James's back providing some of the warmth he felt. On the other side, James thought it might be someone's leg. In such close quarters with other people, James hesitated in getting up. He did not want to disturb those around him.

Instead James tried to remember the previous evening. He was sure his step-father would never let this many people stay the night as they did not have enough room, or enough food. This room also somehow felt bigger than the farm house. James vaguely remembered getting up yesterday and getting his mother to make him lunch. After that he had headed out for a walk. He had been looking for adventure and now James was starting to remember that he found it.

The men snoring around him were the men at the table in the tavern, where he had followed Kendrick. The leader of the group had been Cyrus, who was allowing James to join them on the quest for the Stone of Uzree. Today they were going to start early, James was ready to go because he did not have anything, except the lunch his mother had packed him which he had not had a chance to eat the previous day.

The person snoring beside James rolled over and ended up pinning James's shoulder down. James yelped in pain and the person rolled away from him. The snores from all over the room stopped and shuffling started. Someone lit a lantern near James as the person who rolled on to him sat up. Kendrick looked down at James.

"I am sorry," Kendrick said.

"*Everyone might as well get up,*" Cyrus's voice came from the other side of James. James looked up to see that the person on the other side was Cyrus's legs because Cyrus was sitting with his back to the wall. It sounded like everyone was getting up, so James sat up. The room was the same one supper had been served in the night before. The table was even in the same position.

James realized he had been wrapped in a cloak, not a blanket as he thought. It must have belonged to Cyrus, because his was the only missing one. James carefully picked up the cloak and dusted it off before offering it back to Cyrus. Cyrus took it with a nod.

"It is a little early, is it not?" Kendrick said as he stretched.

"Not that early," Cyrus said as he got to his feet, "The boy was already awake and the sun should be up soon. We might as well get going."

"Very well," Kendrick said. He started to pack up.

James did not have anything to pack up, so he stood to the side while everyone else go themselves ready. Cyrus put on his cloak and then was ready as well. The ten men were quickly ready. Kendrick took several minutes longer.

Finally everyone was ready and Cyrus opened the door. The common room of the tavern was silent and dark. The man from the night before was leaning against the counter and sleeping. He jerked awake as the men went passed. Kendrick stopped and paid the man.

Outside the sky was starting to lighten which was enough for the group to make their way out the village gate and along the road, but it was too dark to see once they were into the forest. Fortunately Cyrus brought the lantern with him. James stayed close to him and the light.

The direction they moved away from his step-father's farm so James was content. The farther away from the farm he went the harder time his step-father would have to drag him back to work. Even better James had been invited on this quest where his step-father would not even look for him. If James had still been on his *own, there might have been a chance of his returning, but not now.*

The path went through the forest, sometimes taking the group further into the trees and sometimes taking them to its edge. When they ventured in, it got darker and there were strange noises. When they were closer to the tree's edge, it was lighter and animals could be seen. The group ignored anything not directly in their path. James stayed near Cyrus and the lantern. He felt safer there. Kendrick was near the back of the group, where he spent the time muttering to himself and not paying attention to his surroundings.

The group was going along part of the path through the deep forest when all the light is sucked out of the air. James, at first, thought the lantern had gone out, but he looked and saw that the flame was still going. The group had stopped and out came their weapons. Cyrus handed James the lantern before pushing the boy behind him. James stood still.

Not only was the light vanished but then James noticed sounds fell silent and nothing moved. Even Kendrick had come out of his self-centered musings and was on alert. The men put their backs to each other and created a circle with James in the middle. Everyone was watching and waiting to learn the cause of this sudden stillness. James found himself holding his breath and consciously started to breathe again.

The trees and bushes in front of the group parted to admit the largest horse James had ever seen. It was as black as a moonless night, except for it hooves, mane, tail, and a horn which grew from the middle of its forehead. These were the red, yellow and orange but the colours flickered. The hooves made no noise as the horse walked toward the group. Its eyes were as red as blood, but they gleamed as if reflecting fire.

James felt a fear descend upon him. It paralyzed him and caused his mind to focus on the beast. The eyes taunted him and shot straight through his soul both acknowledging and dismissing him at the same time. It knew him and wanted to destroy him. His death was its one desire and it could have whatever it desired. The men who surrounded him were mere illusions.

You! The word screamed inside James's head. James wanted to clap his hands over his ears and cower, but he had lost his ability to move. The colours on the horse's horn started to spiral up and down. James felt pulled into its spell.

Kendrick stepped between the horse and the group. He had both his walking stick and sword pointed at the animal. James wanted to shout a warning, but his body and his mouth did not work anymore. Kendrick was calling out some words that James did not understand at all. Their strangeness confused James. He wondered if he should recognize them.

The horse reared up to smash Kendrick's head with his front hooves but before they could connect, there was a flash and loud bang. James found himself coughing at the rancid smoke in the air and was surprised he could move again. When the smoke had finally cleared enough, James looked up and saw that the horse was gone. Kendrick was still standing there, though he had put his sword away, and was trying to wave the smoke away. The rest of the men were in the same condition, except Cyrus who stood there as if nothing was wrong.

"What was that?" one of the men finally choked out.

"The beast, Kerr the Black," Kendrick answered, "He is the steward's beast."

"The steward rides a unicorn?" the man asked.

"Evil begets evil," Cyrus answered, "What did you do to him?"

"I sent him away," Kendrick said, "Hopefully in such a way that he cannot come back any time soon."

"Let us go," Cyrus said, "If we are not here when he returns it would be preferable."

James realized the wild creatures were back and making noise. Subdued light replaced the darkness. The men put their weapons away, but Cyrus was slower to sheath his sword. Once his weapon was put away, Cyrus held out his hand for the lantern. James gave it back. Cyrus started forward and around Kendrick. James stayed close to the lantern and the rest of the men followed them. Kendrick came at the back of the group and was soon mumbling to himself.

Waldemar tried to keep his eyes open, but the warmth of his bed and the soothing voice of his mother lulled him to sleep. His eyes closed for the last time and he slipped into sleep.

Waldemar was running down the castle corridor with his friend, Damon. They had been in the kitchens getting a snack until the cook had ushered them out. Now they were off to see if they could get to the top of the tower without anyone noticing. Waldemar and Damon found no one guarding the bottom of the stair, so they headed up them. They were out of breath by the time they reached the top. Waldemar looked toward the door and found a white wolf sitting in front of it.

Waldemar stared at the animal. It was strange to him and yet felt familiar. Damon was gone, and it was just Waldemar and the wolf, but the wolf showed no signs of attacking him. In fact, it was waiting as if to speak with him.

"Yes?" Waldemar asked.

You are in danger, the voice was feminine, from a source you do not expect.

"What do mean?" Waldemar asked.

Your father summoned a demon, the voice said, His blood runs through your veins, and he used it to hold the demon on this side of the portal. The demon was sent back. However, he sent forth another one to cause chaos. Demons thrive on chaos.

"What am I supposed to do?" Waldemar asked.

Beware of everything, the voice replied.

Waldemar woke up. The curtains were still drawn, but his mother's chair was long empty. He did not hear Eldon, who must not have come in yet. Waldemar got out of bed and went to the window. He tugged aside the curtain and found the sun shining its first rays, which meant it was morning.

He let the curtain drop back into place before going to his wardrobe. Eldon had everything folded and put in its proper place. Waldemar rummaged around until he found the trousers he was looking for and pulled them out. Then he put them on before going to the door. Peering out, he saw there was no one in the hallway. Waldemar left his room and was half-way down the hallway before anyone could appear. He reached the junction of two hallways and stopped to check if the coast was clear. There was no one in sight. Waldemar rushed to the next one.

Peeking around the corner, Waldemar saw Weldon and the castle steward coming down the hallway. Waldemar snuck into the nearest door, which was an empty guard room, and closed the door most of the way.

"Are you sure of what you saw?" Weldon's voice asked.

"I definitely know what I saw," the castle steward answered.

"Where do you think it went?" Weldon asked.

"I think it headed up," the castle steward answered, "I tried to tell the captain of the guard, but he did not believe me."

"He is still new to the job," Weldon said, "He has not seen what you and I have seen. We have to catch it before he will believe us."

"Let us just check on Waldemar before we get too worried about catching the thing," the castle steward said. They rounded the corner and continued down the hallway.

"It is still early in the morning," Weldon said, "He

should still be in bed. We should check in with Arabella as well."

"Good idea," the castle steward said.

They got far enough down the hallway that Waldemar thought he was safe. He slipped out of the closet and headed down the hallway Weldon and the castle steward had come up. He reached the stairs and used the railing as a slide to get to the bottom as fast as he could. He landed with a running start and headed toward the kitchen.

Damon was waiting outside the kitchen for Waldemar. He had two bundles in his hands.

"Here is breakfast," Damon held out one bundle to Waldemar.

"Thank you," Waldemar said as he took the bundle. He unwrapped it and started eating the bread from inside.

"The castle steward is looking for you," Damon said.

"So, is the Duke," Waldemar said, "I saw them, but if they see me I would not be able to go with you today."

"As long as I do not get in trouble," Damon said, "My father told me if I get in trouble again, I would not be allowed to come with him ever again."

"I will take the blame," Waldemar said. He took another bite of the bread before stuffing the rest into his pocket.

"If you say so," Damon said.

"Let us get out of here," Waldemar said. They went into the kitchen, being careful to stay out of people's way, and headed to the door to the courtyard. Outside were several other children of servants waiting for them. When Waldemar and Damon joined them, they headed for the marketplace.

WELDON AND THE CASTLE STEWARD GO IN SEARCH OF A DEMON

The door to Waldemar's room was open when Weldon and the castle steward reached it. Weldon reached out to push it the rest of the way when the door across the hall opened. Both men turned to see Arabella step out of her room and close the door behind her.

"Good morning," Arabella said, "I thought I should try to get up before my son."

"It appears you are too late," Weldon said, "We were just about to check on him."

Weldon entered Waldemar's room, and the other two followed him. The bed was indeed empty, but the boy had not been taken as the wardrobe had been riffled through.

"What is going on?" Arabella asked as she looked around the room. Everything else was as it should have been.

"A demon has been spotted on the castle grounds," the castle steward said.

"Like the one Hillel was getting advice from?" Arabella asked.

"No," the castle steward answered, "It is a different one."

"We have not identified it yet, so we do not know what danger it presents," Weldon said, "We came up to check on Waldemar, just in case."

"If the demon is on the castle grounds, what else could it be after but my son?" Arabella said, "He needs to be found."

"The castle steward and I will keep looking for the demon," Weldon said, "We will send up a guard to help you search for Waldemar. If we find the demon and deal with it, then Waldemar will not be harmed. If you find him, then we can put protection in place to keep him safe."

"Very well," Arabella said, "Send up the guard. I will start looking through the rooms on this floor before heading down to the kitchen."

"We will do so right away," the castle steward said with a bow.

Weldon and the castle steward left Arabella in Waldemar's room and headed down the stairs. The Captain of the guard and three guards were standing inside the castle entrance.

"You asked for a search party," the captain of the guard said when Weldon and the castle steward reached him.

"Yes," Weldon said, "We need to find this demon before it does something we will regret."

"These three can help," the captain of the guard said.

"Well, two of them can," Weldon said.

"Arabella is searching for Waldemar," the castle steward said, "One should go up and help her. She is looking through the rooms around her and Waldemar's rooms."

"Help her," the captain of the guard pointed to the guard on his right. The guard gave a nod before heading up the stairs.

"Thank you," the castle steward said.

"The other two can help you," the captain of the guard said, "Though I doubt you will find anything." He turned and went out the door. The guardsmen looked at the castle steward and Weldon for directions.

"Either of you believe in demons?" Weldon asked. Both nodded.

"Good," Weldon said, "The one we are looking for is about six feet tall and thin. Its skin is white with black patches along its body. Both fingers and toes are long with claws. It has two eyes in its head but seems to lack a mouth. We need to find it fast if we are going to get rid of it."

"Is Lady Rana currently in the capital?" the guardsman on the left asked.

"No, she is supposed to be on her way back today," Weldon answered, "Otherwise we would get help from Eustace in hunting this thing down."

"Where should we start, Duke Weldon?" the other guardsman asked.

"You two search from the top down," Weldon said, "Starting with the tower. We will start at the bottom and work our way up."

"Yes, Duke Weldon," the guardsmen said before they headed off.

"The dungeon?" the castle steward asked. He looked like there was a bitter taste in his mouth.

"Yes," Weldon answered, "I do not like going down there either, but it is a place a demon might hide."

"Okay, let us go," the castle steward said after taking a deep breath.

They headed for the stairs down to the door. Outside the door was a lit torch. Weldon opened the door as the castle steward took the torch down from its bracket. It was dark down there because there was no place for the light to come in. The castle steward used the torch to light one inside the door before Weldon took it down for his use. The first room was large with plenty of torture devices hanging off the walls. On the far side of the room here was another door that led to a similar room. To the left and right, doorways were leading to hallways, which was where the cells were.

Weldon went along one hallway while the castle steward went along the other hallway. Each cell contained a bed and a bucket, but there had not been any prisoners down here since King Proster did a clean out. The cells had been cleaned out as well, so there was nothing in any of the cells except a bed and a bucket. Weldon still felt like there were spirits around, wandering lost and waiting for the Great Reclamation, and it made him feel nervous.

He went down the hallway, checking every cell for any sign of demon activity. Each cell was as it should have been. Weldon reached the end and found the last cell to have a closed door. The doors in this hallway were steel doors with only a small slot for food to be passed to the prisoner. The hallway the castle steward was searching had doors that were just bars and not solid steel. Likely the person who built the prison felt the need to have different security depending on the prisoner. However, since all the other doors along this hallway were open, this one should have been as well.

Weldon pulled on it and found the door was not locked. It opened to a cell looking like all the others, except for a bundle of rags and bones. Curious, Weldon went into the cell and knelt down by the pile. He did not remember any records about anyone being down here since Proster let everyone out. All others who would have ended up down here had been sent to the mines to work off their crimes there. The pile looked old and there was nothing left, except clothing and bones. Weldon stood up and saw something glint as he did so. He pushed aside some of the pile with his foot. Near the bottom of the pile, where it could barely be seen between things, was an amulet. It was round and made of gold with a ruby set in the centre. Weldon reached in and picked it up. There was a gold chain as if it was supposed to be worn around the neck.

"Weldon?" the castle steward called from the end of the hallway.

"In here," Weldon called back. There was no dust or dirt anywhere on the amulet, but there seemed to be a spark glowing from the centre of the ruby. It was slightly mesmerizing and Weldon felt like he should put the amulet away before the castle steward got there, but he fought the urge.

The castle steward reached the doorway and looked in. Weldon looked up at him.

"Did you know there was anything left down here?" Weldon asked.

"No," the castle steward answered, "I had heard a rumour from the man who held my position previous that someone had been left down here, but I thought it was only a story."

"Why were they left down here?" Weldon asked.

"According to the story, King Proster feared the man," the castle steward answered, "But I do not recall King Proster fearing anything or anyone."

"I wonder if anyone would recognize this," Weldon held up the amulet, "Because if someone does, we could return the body for burial."

"I can put out a notice about," the castle steward said, "When we are finished with the search for the demon."

"That should do fine," Weldon said slipping the amulet into his pocket. He stepped out of the cell and closed the door. Then he and the castle steward headed to the large room.

"Did you find anything?" Weldon asked the castle steward.

"There is nothing down here," the castle steward said.

"Then we better head up a floor," Weldon said. They reached the larger room and Weldon put the torch out before putting it back on the wall. They left the dungeon and closed the door behind them. The castle steward put the torch back in it bracket before they continued up the stairs.

The guardsman had found Arabella opening doors and checking each room for Waldemar, but since he did not know where she had checked he waited until she was finished. It was not long. She came towards where he was standing.

"I was sent to help you," the guardsman said with a bow.

"Well, he is not up here," Arabella said, "We might as well start down in the kitchen and the dining room."

"Yes, Lady Arabella," the guardsman bowed before following her down the stairs. Arabella headed straight to the kitchen. Both she and the guardsman stepped into the kitchen but did not go farther than that because everyone was busy trying to get breakfast ready. The cook was busy, but his assistant was able to leave her job and come over to them.

"Yes, Lady Arabella?" the cook's assistant asked.

"Have you seen Waldemar?" Arabella asked.

"I did not see him specifically," the cook's assistant answered, "But a group of children went through here half an hour ago. He may have been with them."

"Did you see which way they were headed?" Arabella asked.

"I think they were headed for the marketplace," the cook's assistant answered.

"Thank you," Arabella said.

"You are welcome, Lady Arabella," the cook's assistant curtsied and then went back to work.

Arabella and the guardsman left the kitchen. She headed to the nearest door out to the courtyard and looked around. There were no children in sight. If there had been a group of them, then they were gone already.

"Would you like me to go to the marketplace and look for him?" the guardsman asked.

"No," Arabella answered, "He will be back this evening with the rest of them. If the demon is hanging around the castle, then he will be safer there than here. You should be helping in the search for the demon anyway."

"Lady Arabella?" the guardsman asked. Arabella looked at him. The guardsman was a young man; likely he had not been a guard for more than a couple years. She realized he had not heard of the demon, who had been filling her husband's head with lies, and did not believe they even existed.

"The demon is out there," Arabella implored the guardsman, "And is a danger to this whole kingdom if it is not found and disposed of. A demon is not an imaginary creature from a fairy tale, it is the realization of nightmares."

The guardsman could see the truth in her eyes and she watched the fear creep into his. He did not need to see one for himself and Arabella sincerely hoped he would never have to, but he did believe her.

"I will go see where the captain needs me," the guardsman bowed before going off. Arabella watched him. She was sorry to scare him, but if there was another demon around then it was necessary. Arabella turned and went back inside. There was nothing she could do, except find someplace safe to sit and worry about her son.

The captain of the guards had finished supervising formations and was on his way to the stable to check on the stable boy, who had been skipping off work to visit the cook's daughter. She also had other things she should have been doing. The captain of the guard had been keeping tabs on them and trying to keep them apart. The cook tried to keep his daughter inside and busy, but with his own job taking up so much time it was difficult to keep track of her. The stable boy was an orphan who the captain of the guard had taken in and given a job in the stables. Both were about twelve and already getting too close to adulthood.

A noise from behind the stables stopped the captain of the guard from going inside. Since there was nothing behind the stables to make noise, the captain of the guard figured it had to be the children avoiding their responsibilities. He headed around the stable set and determined to give them both a lecture.

The captain of the guard stopped in his tracks at the sight of what was behind the stables. The cook's daughter was lying unconscious with a creature bending over her. It was white with black spots stretching over various parts of its body. It fingers were twice the length of any human's and had claws that looked sharp. The toes of the creature were similar. It had two black eyes in a human-shaped face on top of a body that looked like sticks. The lower half of the thing's face separated and showed two sets of sharp teeth. It was lowering its mouth toward the cook's daughter with saliva dripping out and down.

Forcing all thoughts from his head, the captain of the guard pulled his sword and with a shout started toward the creature. It looked up at him and closed its mouth, which made the mouth disappear. The creature backed away from the cook's daughter as the captain of the guard ran at it. The wall around the courtyard stopped it from going any further back, but when the captain of the guard's sword came close to it, the creature disappeared. The captain of the guard came up short and looked around, but it was nowhere in sight. The only things he saw was the stable boy with a bloody gash on the head sitting with his back to the stable. The boy's eyes were closed.

The captain of the guard used his sword to continue toward the wall he had the creature backing into to see if it just turned invisible, but he did not come across anything. He put his sword away for the moment because it did not look like it was going to be any use. He went over and checked on the cook's daughter. She was breathing and did not appear to have been harmed. The captain of the guard went over to the stable boy and checked on him. The gash was large and still bleeding. His breathing was also ragged. The captain of the guard took out his handkerchief and tied it around the stable boy's head making sure to cover the wound.

A groan from behind him caused the captain of the guard to turn around. The cook's daughter was waking up. She slowly sat up and looked around.

"What happened?" she asked the captain of the guard when she saw him.

"I will explain in a minute," he answered, "Right now we need to get both of you into the castle."

"Okay," she said looking confused. She got to her feet and appeared to be stable, so the captain of the guard turned back to the stable boy. He lifted the boy into his arms and headed around the stable with the cook's daughter following him.

When they reached the door, the two guards on either side stared.

"Go get a doctor," the captain of the guard said to the one on the left. The man nodded and hurried off. The other one opened the door to let the group in. The captain of the guard took the boy to a guard room, which was the first door on the left off the hallway that led to the throne room. There were four beds, but no guards because this room was only used when they needed more guards on the front doors.

He placed the stable boy on one bed while the cook's daughter sat down on another one. The captain of the guard removed his handkerchief to see how bad the gash on the stable boy's face was.

"So, what happened?" the cook's daughter asked as she used the sheet to wipe off the saliva which had fallen on her.

"You were attacked," the captain of the guard answered as he wiped away some of the blood to get a better look.

"By what?" the cook's daughter asked.

"A demon," the captain of the guards answered, "It seemed to be very interested in eating you, but when I attacked it disappeared."

"So, it could be around here someplace," the cook's daughter had frozen and she looked scared.

"I do not think it will attack here," the captain of the guard said, "But I really do not know because I have never faced a demon and until I saw it I did not think such a thing existed."

The castle steward and Weldon stepped into the room and saw what was going on.

"It attacked?" Weldon asked.

"Yes," the captain of the guard said, "I scared it off, but it disappeared before I could touch it with my sword."

"We need to step up our search," the castle steward said.

"Once the doctor gets here, I will get as many of the guards searching as I can," the captain of the guards said.

"We send the two up to start with the tower," Weldon said, "We just finished the dungeon. Make sure you sent them out in groups of two."

"I will," the captain of the guard said.

Weldon and the castle steward left the room to continue their search. The guard and the doctor came in. The captain of the guard moved away from the stable boy to give the doctor space and stopped the guard before he could leave.

"I will send someone else to take up your post," the captain of the guard told him, "I want you to stay here and keep watch."

"Yes, sir," the guard said. He took a position by the door as the captain of the guard left the room.

Weldon and the castle steward headed toward the storage rooms to continue their search of any places a demon may make a home.

"Until we find the demon, no one should be wandering around by themselves," Weldon said.

"Then I need to let the housekeeper know, as well as others," the castle steward said, "I do not want them to panic, but a warning to be watchful and stay in groups should be good."

"Go," Weldon said, "I have some quick paperwork to do in my office, as well as sending my clerks home."

"I will find you when I am finished," the castle steward said before going off. Weldon continued toward his office.

He was just about there when he came across Arabella and her handmaiden. Both were headed upstairs but stopped when they saw him.

"Did you find Waldemar?" Weldon asked Arabella.

"He seems to have gone to the marketplace with a group of children," Arabella said, "As worried as I am about it, I believe he might be safer there than here. I heard there was an attack."

"Yes," Weldon said, "I do not know the specifics, but it looked like the stable boy and the cook's daughter were attacked. Likely they were off somewhere by themselves and were easy targets for the demon."

"Are they all right?" Arabella asked.

"She seemed to be, but the stable boy was still unconscious and bleeding from a head wound," Weldon answered, "It is best if no one spends time alone or in out of the way places until the demon is dealt with."

"We will be up in the library," Arabella said, "Hopefully, it will be out of the way of the search, but not someplace the demon is going to go."

"Keep a lantern going," Weldon advised.

"I will," Arabella said. She and her handmaiden proceeded up the stairs. Weldon headed into his office.

Inside his clerks were busy with their paperwork The lower court was on its usual day off, which helped with the search for the demon, but did not mean there was a lack of paperwork needing to be done. The clerks barely glanced up when Weldon entered the room. However when he did not move, they cleaned their quills and looked up at him.

"The work can wait," Weldon said, "Go home until I send word for you to come back and stay together until you are out of the courtyard."

"Is there something wrong?" the clerk on the right asked.

"Yes," Weldon answered, "There is a demon somewhere in the castle and we have not figured out where."

"We will wait for your word," the clerk on the left said. Both of them hurried to clean up. Weldon went to his desk and sat down.

The captain of the guard had guards sent in all directions to search for the demon. Several did not believe demons existed, but the fear in their leader caused them to question their doubts. Everyone did as they were told and everyone had a place to search. Those who were not searching had been assigned specific places or people to keep watch over. Finally, the captain of the guard had sent them all away and headed back into the castle. He went to the room where he had left the stable boy, the cook's daughter, and the doctor. The guard was still as his assigned post.

The doctor was bandaging the stable boy's head while the cook's daughter had not moved. She had wrapped herself in the blanket.

"How is he?" the captain of the guard asked the

doctor.

"He is still alive," the doctor said, "But we will not know more until he wakes up. When it comes to head injuries there can be a lot of things that can go wrong. He may never wake up, or he could be a different person, or something much worse. In the meantime, I stitched up the wound and am putting a dressing on it. I need to get to an appointment I had set up and then I will come back to check on him."

"Very well," the captain of the guard said. He looked at the cook's daughter before turning to the door. She was starting to close her eyes and fall asleep. The captain of the guard left the room and headed for the kitchen.

The kitchen workers were cleaning up from making breakfast, which was being kept warm until enough people gathered in the dining room to eat breakfast. The cook and his assistant were sitting by the door to the courtyard and enjoying the fresh breeze coming in. They both looked up at the captain of the guard as he approached.

"Is there something wrong?" the cook asked, "We have seen quite a few guardsmen this morning and no one seems to be sitting down for breakfast."

"There is a demon somewhere on the castle grounds," the captain of the guard answered, "People are being asked to go places in groups and the guards are helping to find it."

"No one is likely to leave the kitchen until people are ready to sit down for breakfast," the cook said, "Anything else?"

"Yes," the captain of the guard said, "Your daughter and the stable boy were attacked behind the stable. She is fine, but he may or may not wake up."

"Where is she?" the cook asked as he got to his feet.

"The guard room by the entrance," the captain of the guard answered, "But I do not think she should leave yet because I have a guard stationed in the room to keep them safe."

"That is fine," the cook said, "I just want to make sure she is all right."

The captain of the guard watched him go off before heading out to the courtyard to see if anyone had anything to report.

At noon, people were allowed to gather in the dining room to eat. The cook served what had been made for breakfast and kept warm. The guards only stopped briefly, even though the whole castle grounds had been checked and nothing had been found. The captain of the guard reorganized and sent everyone back out to look again. Weldon and the castle steward had finished their search and joined the captain of the guard at his table. They ate before giving their reports.

"The guards have found nothing," the captain of the guard said, "I have sent them all back out to search again."

"We have not come up with any trace of it," Weldon said, "I would almost say it is not here, but where else could it be?"

"No one has been able to tell me where King Waldemar is," the captain of the guard said.

"Arabella looked for him this morning," Weldon said, "She found evidence that he was headed for the marketplace with several other children. It was felt that he was safer there than to be brought back here. After all, if a demon showed up in the market place there would be a panic and we would hear about it."

"That is probably true," the captain of the guard said,

"Though with no trace of the demon here in the castle or anywhere on the grounds, we might have to turn our attention to the rest of the city."

"Somehow I do not think the demon has left the castle grounds," Weldon said, "I may be wrong, but my instinct says it is still here."

"Well, no one has found a trace of it since the attack this morning," the captain of the guard said.

"It cannot hide forever," the castle steward said.

There was a scream from somewhere outside the dining room. The guards, who were there hurried to the door. Weldon, the castle steward, and the captain of the guard jumped up and rushed toward the sound. The scream had been cut off, but it they figured it came from the front hallway. The three men reached it in time to see the demon dragging the cook's daughter away from the room with the guard chasing after it. Swords came out as everyone else who had come from the dining room charged. Just before the guard's sword reached the demon, it disappeared. Everyone stopped and stared; then search around them, but the demon was gone and with it the cook's daughter.

Weldon, the castle steward, and the captain of the guard stood back where they had stopped.

"It did that same thing when I attacked it before," the captain of the guard said, "We are going to have to figure out how to stop it from doing that and soon."

"We also better figure out where it is hiding," the castle steward said, "And soon if we want to get the cook's daughter back."

"We have searched all the places a demon would usually hide," Weldon said, "And the rest of the castle grounds have been thoroughly checked over. Where else can we look?"

"How long until Lady Rana gets back?" the castle steward asked.

"Tomorrow some time," Weldon answered.

"I suggest until then, we are stuck going over the same ground and hope for a different result," the castle steward said, "Because I do not know where else to look."

THE PRINCE RETURNS, THE STORY IS CONTINUED, AND THEN SOME MORE IS READ ON REQUEST

Waldemar and the rest of the children, who had gone to the marketplace for the day, arrived shortly after supper would have been served, but they were not worried because they had all gotten something for supper at the marketplace. By the time they slipped into the courtyard the search had died down though all the guards were still alert for any possible sign of the demon. The rest of the children went off to find their parents or guardians, who would be getting off work and be heading home. Only a few actually lived in the castle.

Waldemar was alone by the time he had gone through the kitchen and was sneaking up to his room. It was usual and aside from having to go around a few extra guards, Waldemar did not notice anything out of the ordinary going on. When he reached his room, Waldemar expected to see everything tidied and his bed clothes being put out by Eldon. Instead, everything looked exactly as he left it this morning and Eldon, along with any sign of his cleaning, was nowhere in sight.

Shrugging his shoulders, Waldemar got out his school books and sat down at the desk in the corner. He skimmed through his lessons for the day and did a few of the exercises. It was enough for someone to think he actually sat there and worked on it during the day.

When he heard someone coming down the hallway, Waldemar closed the books and headed towards the bed. He slipped his trousers off and tossed them into the laundry pile before getting into bed. By the time the door opened, he was sitting there with the blanket pulled up to his chest.

His mother entered the room and looked around. When she saw him in bed, she headed for her chair.

"I thought it was about time for us to read a chapter," Arabella said with a smile.

"I am ready," Waldemar said.

"Then let us begin," Arabella said as she picked up the book and made herself comfortable, "Chapter two."

The city gates stood in front of the group as they waited in the line-up for the guards to check papers. James had to tip his head back to see the top of them. They had intricate designs carved into them above the ten foot mark. The walls went as far as the eye could see to either side of the gates. The whole city was inside the walls, there were not any farm fields to evident out in the country although James doubted there were any farms connected to the city.

The line-up moved along with the guards checking everyone's papers and finally the group reached the guards. Cyrus kept a hand on James's shoulder as he handed his papers to the guard. The guard looked them over before peering down at James.

"The age of the boy?" the guard asked Cyrus.

"In his tenth year," Cyrus answered. James wanted to correct

him, but realized that Cyrus was lying to get him passed the guards. At fourteen, James should already have papers, but his stepfather had never bothered to take him to get registered. James hoped the guard would believe Cyrus and he would be allowed to enter.

"Very well," the guard said handing the papers back to Cyrus and then turned to the next man. Cyrus kept his hand on James's shoulder as they entered the gates. They stepped to one side to wait for the rest of the men.

The men did not take long going through the gates and join them. All the papers were checked and nothing caused the guards to stop them. Being adventurers was not illegal and all ten men tended to avoid larger settlements where trouble would be more likely to find them.

Cyrus led the way down the cobblestone street. The residents of the city got out of his way as if they were worried he would strike them down. James was able to slip in behind Cyrus rather than walk beside him. Having someone else walking in front helped James feel safer as many of the residents did not seem happy to see the group.

The group went around the corner and the sign for an inn came into view. Cyrus led the group to the door and inside. The main room only had one man sitting in the corner, though the owner came in as the last man in the group closed the door. The man sitting in the corner did not look up from his meal. The owner looked over the group and did not look to happy to see them.

"Can I help you?" the owner asked.

"Food and rooms," Cyrus answered.

The owner looked like he wanted to refuse them. "Of course, sirs," the owner said, "Seat yourselves and I will bring out the food while the rooms are readied." He gave a slight bow before going back into the other room. Cyrus sat down at the long table with James sliding next to him and the rest joining them. Every other day the group was usually chatting among themselves, but today they were quiet as they waited for the food to arrive. It was almost as if they were waiting for someone to attack rather than serve.

The owner came out with a tray of dishes and started handing them down the table. He only had six dishes, so it did not take long. The owner checked over how many more still needed to be fed. He counted the bowls, just about missing James as he went passed. After a moment, he recounted and this time he made sure he counted James. Then the owner went off. A few minutes passed and he came back with the rest of the dishes. Once they were handed out, he disappeared into the back again.

The man sitting by himself finished his meal and then slipped out. James saw Cyrus noticed as well. The rest of the group were busy eating. Each dish had two scoopfuls of stew in the bottom with a thin slice of bread. Drinks had not been delivered, but James suspected the owner did that because Cyrus had asked for food and had not mentioned drink. None of the men spoke about it. James poked at the stew and it bounced back. The lumps were unidentifiable, though James supposed some of them were vegetable matter. He doubted any of it was meat. If he had wanted cooking anywhere near this bad he would have stayed at the farm.

Cyrus and the rest of the men ate as if it was the only food they had seen in a while. James tried a bite, but found it gag worthy. He took a piece of bread and put it into his mouth. It was the worst thing he had ever tasted in his life and made his mother's bread seem delicious, which it was not. James was very careful to try not to be obvious as he spat the bread back into the bowl. No one said anything as James pushed the bowl away.

The owner peeked around the corner to look in on the group, but quickly disappeared again. It seemed as if the owner was hoping they would disappear, rather than just checking to see if they were finished eating. James wondered how a city could be so unfriendly to a small group of men who were just looking for a place to stay for the night. What was the point of an inn if no one was supposed to stay?

Bowls were being scrapped and the last mouthfuls were being swallowed when the door to the inn opened. Two guards and a man in fancy clothes stepped into the main room. They looked over the room before coming to stand near the table. The owner gave a final peek then hastily departed. The man in the fancy clothes studied the group for a moment before going towards Cyrus.

Cyrus looked up from his final bite. He sized up the guards before turning his attention to the man in the fancy clothes. Cyrus obviously did not think any of them were a danger to the group as he did not reach for a weapon, but merely pushed his bowl away.

"I am Lord Lorenzo," the man in the fancy clothes announced, "King Tezacoati sent me as a messenger as soon as he heard of your arrival. He offers proper food and lodging for the night at the palace."

"And if we refuse?" Cyrus's tone was light and non-defensive.

"You can stay here," Lord Lorenzo answered, "Though you are not very welcome here."

Cyrus seemed to contemplate the offer, while the rest of the men waited for him make the decision. James sat quietly, but he was not getting good feelings off Lord Lorenzo and the guards. He was sure that they were leading into a trap.

"I think," Cyrus started but paused briefly, "We will accept the king's offer."

"Wonderful," Lord Lorenzo said, "Follow us." He went to stand near the guards. The men waited until Cyrus nodded, then they got ready. Cyrus leaned down to James.

"Keep your head down," Cyrus whispered before straightening up, "Let us go."

The group got to their feet and followed Lord Lorenzo out of the inn with the guards trailing behind them. The walk felt like it was up hill all the way, but likely it was that way just for the last few streets. Lord Lorenzo set a quick pace considering his clothing and the group kept their pace to match. The guards followed along being more preoccupied with keeping the group together than worried about their speed. James had gotten used to walking with the men and the pace did not bother him at all. The residents still avoided the group as if they might carry a plague or something worse.

James was paying attention to where they were going when a girl caught his attention. She was standing at the entrance to an alley way and studying the crowd as if she was looking for something specific. She wore a tattered red skirt, a shirt that was a couple sizes too large, a vest with matched the skirt, and a bandanna to keep her hair out of her face. Her hair was blonde and curly, while her eyes were a mesmerizing blue. She was dirty from living in places not fit for human habitation, but her pale skin shone. She appeared to be about his age, though she could have been older if she suffered from mal-nutrition. James did not miss a step, but he watched her until he no longer could see her. She never noticed him, likely because he was between men with cloaks that swept the ground and seemed to hide everything else.

They reached the palace quite quickly. The building sat in the center of the city and was bigger than the village where Kendrick had taken James when they joined the group. Around the building itself were plenty of gardens with flowers, fruit trees, and hedge mazes. There were several carriages parked along the drive to the palace with drivers taking care of horses and footmen in discussion groups. All of them watched the group go by before going back to their gossip. In the gardens nobility could be seen frolicking around and laughing. If any glanced in the direction of the drive they did not bother to stop and look at the group. At the door guards flanked the entrance, but they did not stop the group as Lord Lorenzo led them inside.

The inside of the palace was expensively decorated with gold, silver, purple, and the occasional hint of bronze. The walls, floors, and ceiling were covered with detailed painting. The rug that went down the middle of the hallway was of the finest fabrics as were the curtains which blocked the view of rooms going off this hallway. At the end the hallway curtains were open and showed a large, well-lit room, which could only be the throne room. This room continued the theme set by the hallway with the paintings and expensive furnishings and decorations. There was a raised dais at the far end of the room with a dozen steps up to the thrones which sat on it. Both thrones were gold with precious gems embedded all over it. The room itself was large enough to parade an army, but today was filled with nobility in their decorative gowns and expensive suits. They all stepped out of the way as the group came forward.

Lord Lorenzo led the way across the room to a line several feet from the dais. He stopped there and bowed. Cyrus followed his lead and the rest of the men did so as well. James bowed near Cyrus because he was tall enough to be noticed if he stayed standing.

The king was slouched in his throne. He wore purple silk with gold trim and in his hand he played with a gold scepter. His hair was brown, curly and must have fallen to his waist. His piercing blue eyes shone with intelligence, but his too big mouth seemed to suggest folly resided here as well. The gold crown was slightly tilted on his head with the middle gemstone off to one side. Beside him was the queen, she sat straight with her hands folded in her lap. Her skin was porcelain with pale blue eyes and blonde hair pulled back in a fancy hair style which included pearls and diamonds. She wore a long gown the same colour as her eyes with white accessories. Her tiara was fixed into her hair and made of silver with a large diamond in the center along with two smaller ones on either side of it.

"The strangers, as you requested," Lord Lorenzo announced.

"Thank you," the king said as he waved Lord Lorenzo off. Lord Lorenzo went to stand in the crowd with the rest of the nobility. The king was silent as he looked over the group. He reached over to the table nearby and picked up a goblet. After taking a drink, he put it back, all without looking at it.

"The leader may rise," the king said. Cyrus got to his feet. He was in front of James, so James could no longer see the king but he did not dare move in case it drew attention to him. He would have to settle for merely listening.

"You are the group which is helping the wizard Kendrick?" the king asked.

"We are, Your Highness," Cyrus answered.

"Then we welcome you to our home and hope you enjoy our hospitality," the king said, "Our city is not as welcoming to guests as we would like, but I assure you that you will get plenty here. Plenty to eat and plenty of rest."

"Thank you for your hospitality," Cyrus said with a bow.

"Wyatt will show you to your rooms," the king said signaling for someone to come forward. A page stepped forward and bowed to the king before turning to the group. Everyone got to their feet before following Wyatt out the side door. This led to a hallway which was much darker than the throne room, but had enough light for the group to see. The paintings on these walls did not appear to be finished and the number of torch mounts were lacking so the area was darker. The rug was gone completely and the group walked right on the stone of the floor, which was in the same condition as the walls. There were no curtained doorways along here.

Wyatt led the way along this hallway until it came to a junction, at which point he turned left, and followed this hallway. This hallway was brighter as the torches were mounted at proper intervals. The rug was laid in this hallway and the painting was finished. There were also plenty of curtained doorways along here. Wyatt did not stop at any of these doorways, but walked passed them. Occasionally James could hear music or giggling from behind the curtains, but the fabric made it impossible to see what was going on in those rooms.

At the end of that hallway was a large open area with a grand staircase taking up most of the space. There were some doors behind the staircase, but those who were guests were supposed to ignore those and go up the stairs. This room had several windows along the wall at the top of the staircase where it went in two directions. Wyatt led the way up the stairs and to the left. This led into another hallway, but the walls were merely painted one colour and it lacked any of the fanciness from previous hallways. The windows continued along the right wall as they went giving them light without needing torches.

It was halfway down this hallway that Wyatt stopped and opened a door. This was also the first doorway along this hallway and the next one must have been far enough down that they could not see it. Wyatt stepped back so the group could get in and see what was inside. There was a main room with plenty of furniture and tables for a group twice as large as this one. Off the main room was ten rooms, which from the open doors, appeared to be bedrooms. Each one had a cushy bed and a wash stand.

"Make yourselves comfortable," Wyatt said, "Supper will be in the dining room in half an hour. Also if you need anything, just ring the bell." Wyatt pointed to the cord beside the door. He gave a bow before heading back down the hallway. The men shuffled into the main room and Cyrus closed the door. Everyone was silent as they studied their surroundings. James saw Cyrus hold up a crystal ball the size of an acorn. He studied for a minute as he moved it around as if shining it in various corners of the room. Finally he nodded and put it away.

"No one is listening," Cyrus said.

The silence broken the men began to talk to each other as they sorted out who was going to sleep where. The room which should have gone to Cyrus was given instead to James, as Cyrus claimed not to need a room but would keep watch in the main room. James put his small bundle down on the floor beside the wash stand before climbing up on the bed. It was a good distance from the floor and filled with something soft which gave easily when pressed. Sitting there on the edge, James was hesitant in going farther on to the bed because he was not sure about his chances on making it out. The blankets were just as soft as the rest of it and inviting after walking all day after and a night lying on the ground. However, James knew the day was not over and going to sleep would have him miss supper. Since he did not eat the stew from the inn, he was really hungry. He wondered what kind of things the king would have for them to eat, since it appeared they would be eating with him.

James had not closed the door and could hear the men gathering in the main room. They had obviously dealt with their stuff and wanted to discuss what was next. A few were talking about their uncertainty about the king's intentions. At least one wanted to leave and find somewhere safer to take the night. Cyrus shot that suggestion down as it was unlikely they could leave without the king finding out and they still had to get out of the city. It was better to go to supper and see what happened from there. This quieted some of the grumbling, but there was still some uncertainty. Cyrus suggested that everyone be careful and watchful.

James checked his knife, which was strapped to his forearm, and it was just as he thought it. He carefully got off the bed and went over to his bundle. James took out the dagger Cyrus had given him. He strapped it to his lower leg. Standing up he walked around for a minute to make sure that it was comfortable and was not noticeable. Then James joined the others. No one noticed him, except maybe Cyrus, who gave no indication he did. They all continued talking about whether they were in danger or not.

A knock came at the door and everyone fell silent. Cyrus went over and opened it. Wyatt stood there.

"If you will follow me, I will take you to the dining room," Wyatt said.

"Very well," Cyrus said before stepping out of the room. James followed close behind him and the rest of the men came behind at their own pace. Wyatt led the way back down the stairs and through the hallways to the one that was not finished, where they turned left on to it and went along the part they had not visited. This hallway went straight to the dining room.

The dining room was long and narrow with dramatic paintings covering the walls and ceiling. The floor was marble. In the middle of the room was a table that ran most of the length of the room with chairs all the way down either side. Most of the chairs were made of silver with silk cushions, except the chairs at each end of the table which were made of gold. The king sat at one end and the queen sat at the other end. Many of the chairs were already filled.

Wyatt signalled for the group to sit in the empty chairs on the left side of the queen. Cyrus sat closest with James taking the seat on the other side from the queen. The rest of the men settled themselves in the chairs along the line. Other nobility came in behind the group and settled in their chairs. Wyatt stood beside the wall behind the group similar to other servants in the room. No one sat at the other side of the queen, but all of them gathered at the king's end of the table.

People stopped entering and they all settled themselves in their chairs. The king slouched in his chair as he waited for everyone to finish shuffling, while the queen sat properly with her eyes on the table in front of her. When everyone was ready, the servants brought in the food. This food looked much better than what was served at the inn and James felt his stomach grumble with hunger. He checked to see if anyone noticed the noise, but it appeared as if they had not. James waited with everyone else until the king started to eat, then everyone picked up their forks.

As he ate, James noticed the queen. She sat there and ate dainty bites one at a time. Her eyes continued to stare at the table in front of her and her eyes showed a sadness James had not seen earlier.

"Are you okay, Your Majesty?" Cyrus's voice was soft and James almost missed hearing the question. He thought for sure that the queen had not heard it at all as her eyes continued to focus on the table. Then her eyes flicked over to Cyrus before going back to the table. Nothing else moved.

"No," Her mouth moved so little James almost looked around to see who spoke, "I live a cursed life because of my husband and there is nothing I can do about it."

"What is the curse?" Cyrus asked.

"I will never bear the king a son," the queen answered, "Every child I have given birth to have been a princess, which he rejects and hides away. The search goes on for the cure, but he will not reveal

why he is cursed."

"Princesses can become queens, who rule just as effectively as kings," Cyrus said.

"The king refuses to acknowledge any of the princesses," the queen answered, 'They reach twelve and they disappear. I know he sends them away, but I know not where. I refused to bear him any more children until the curse is lifted and he came close to banning me from the kingdom, but in the end respected my decision. If I was not going to have a prince and he took away my children then there was no point having anymore."

"How many are gone?" Cyrus asked.

"Thirteen," the queen answered.

"We are on a quest to find other lost items," Cyrus said, "We can look for them."

"If you can I would appreciate it," the queen said, "But I doubt you will have the time to put towards such as search."

"We will do what we can," Cyrus said. James saw that the queen still believed there was no hope for her problem to be solved, though he did not understand why. Cyrus had just offered her some hope that the group could find her daughters and she seemed as if she would be happy to have them back, yet she did not hope.

Cyrus said nothing more to her and she did not reply. The men on the other side of James had gotten comfortable enough to talk among themselves, but as there were limited people close enough they did not socialize with members of the king's court. James finished all the food on his plate, but did not feel the need to have anymore.

When everyone was done eating, the king and queen got up. They went out the door on the other side of the room together as everyone else watched. As soon as they were gone, everyone got up to leave. Wyatt moved up to lead the group out of the dining room. Cyrus followed him with the rest of the group trailing him. James stayed close to Cyrus.

Wyatt led them back up to their suite and left them there. He did not give them instructions to stay in the room, but none of the group felt like investigating how far their welcome reached. Instead they all went into their rooms to get an early start on their sleep so they could leave as early as possible the next morning. James went into his room and climbed up on the bed. He had thought about removing his weapons and other such to get ready for bed, but somehow he did not feel safe in this place without them. So, he laid down and let the bed surround him. It would be hard to get out of in the morning, but James was tired and not too worried about it. With the bed embracing him, James could do nothing else but close his eyes. Sleep closed in on James and he was quickly out.

The night definitely was not over, especially if darkness was any indication. James did know he was no longer in the soft bed, or his own room. The snoring was only part of it. James opened his eyes and found a low level of light, which came from a doorway nearby. It showed the walls and ceiling were made of stone blocks, which did not match the smooth walls of the room James had fallen asleep in. James tried to sit up, but there was an arm over his chest. He pushed it off and sat up. All around him the members of the group were lying on the stone floor, except Cyrus who was sitting up beside the door. His eyes were open, but out of focus, which meant he was not conscious of whatever was around him.

James got to his feet and carefully made his way to Cyrus. No one else was awake. The room was circular with the doorway being the only exit. Outside the door James could see a stone hallway, but not much else. James went to Cyrus and shook his shoulder, but got no response. Calling Cyrus's name, James kept shaking his shoulder. There was still no response.

There was a noise from the hallway. James looked up, but did not see anything. It sounded like cloth sliding along the floor. It got closer for a moment and then got further away, like it had passed by the doorway but James had not seen anything. Then the sound got too far away and James could not hear it anymore.

James shook Cyrus harder, but he did not get any response.

Nothing caused any changes with Cyrus. James clapped his hands together in front of Cyrus's face. Cyrus blinked once and focused on James. James moved back to give Cyrus room.

Cyrus got to his feet and looked around. James stayed where he had sat down. Cyrus nudged some of the men, but none of them gave any response. They were all alive because they still breathing. Cyrus looked out into the hallway, but apparently did not see anything that made him go out any farther.

"I woke up here," James said, "Where are we?"

"The dungeon under King Tezacoati's palace," Cyrus answered, "Word has gone around that King Tezacoati is in cahoots with the Steward, but I did not know for sure until the queen confirmed it last night."

"Why would King Tezacoati work with the Steward?" James asked, "King Tezacoati usually only worries about his own affairs and ignores other peoples."

"King Tezacoati is feeling his age," Cyrus answered, "He may have a couple hundred years on the rest of us, but in that time he has never produced a male heir to leave his kingdom to and the queen has refused to be bedded every time he thinks he may have found the answer. That all means he is hoping the Steward has some way of reversing the curse in exchange for putting us in his dungeon and not letting us out."

"What is down here?" James asked.

"I do not know," Cyrus answered, "But no one comes out of here alive, or at all."

"So, what do we do now?" James asked.

"We need to wait out the spell holding the rest of the group," Cyrus answered, "Then we make our way carefully to the exit and get out. If we do it right, King Tezacoati will not know we are gone until we have gotten a good distance away."

"How long do you think it will for the spell to wear off?" James asked.

"I do not know," Cyrus answered, "I do not know how long we

were out. It could be a few minutes or several hours." Cyrus sat back down where he had been sitting before.

"Something is out there," James said.

"Very likely," Cyrus replied.

"I heard it," James said.

"We will figure it out," Cyrus said, "Later."

James sat quietly. He nudged the nearest foot, but did not get any response out of the man. Cyrus did not say anything. James thought about doing it until the man woke up, but decided it was not a good idea. Cyrus would probably suggest he stop long before the man woke up.

An echoed knocking sound came from out in the hallway, but it sounded far away. It happened once and did not come again, so it was impossible to tell if it close or far away. James could not tell what had made the sound, or whether he should be worried about it. Cyrus did not appear to be disturbed by the sound.

"Do you think there are rats down here?" James asked.

"I doubt it," Cyrus answered, "Rats are a good food source, so the population is likely to be kept down by whatever does live here."

James tried not to shutter at that thought, but it was hard. He never had liked rats and anything big enough to subsist on them sent a chill down his spine. The sound of cloth had an eerie quality to it that had chilled James and made him want to avoid it. The knocking sound just added to his want to get out of this place. But they would need the team if they hoped to get out of there and that meant waiting for the team to wake up, which meant accepting strange noises for the time being.

There was a screeching like rock being scrapped along rock. It went on for a full minute before stopping. James tried to sit quietly and coolly as Cyrus, but his heart was going as fast as a rabbit which was causing his hands to shake. He sat on them to keep Cyrus from noticing, though it was likely Cyrus had noticed and just did not comment.

One of the men rolled over onto another one causing both to curse and sit up. In untangling themselves, they hit the person near them, who groaned. The noise they made started to wake everyone else up. As they woke up, the men realized they were not in the same place as they had fallen asleep. They looked to Cyrus for an answer, but he waited until everyone was awake and paying attention before explaining what he knew. There was grumbling and a few muttered I-told-you-we-should-not-have-stayed, while an inventory was being taken. The men had slept in their cloaks with their weapons on, so aside from the bags that had been carried, everything was there. With that established, Cyrus suggested they head out. No one saw any reason to stay put, so everyone got ready to move out.

Cyrus took the lead and James was right behind him. The rest of the group took their positions behind. The hallway was stone from top to bottom. The floor had bits of debris scattered along the edges with a clear path down the middle. There were torches at regular intervals along the walls, so the group never had any problems with light. Most of what littered the floor was pieces of rock and sand, there were no bones or cloth or anything which suggested human remains. James took that as a good thing, but it made him wonder what happened to the people who preceded them.

The hallway curved this way and that with very few straight stretches. The group walked for several minutes before they came across a doorway. It was a narrow and there was no light within the room. However, there was plenty coming from the torches in the hallway to see. The room was round with a statue as its only occupant. The stone statue was of a girl about eleven or twelve years old. She wore a long flowing gown and had her hair in loose waves going down her back. Her facial features were similar to King Tezacoati's features.

"Looks like one of the daughters," one of the men said.

"Probably the oldest," Cyrus replied.

"Why the oldest?" the man asked.

"*She is the first one we have found,*" *Cyrus answered, "And the king probably put them down here in order because he was not sure how many rooms he would need.*"

"*Should we let the queen know after we get out of here?*" *one of the other men asked.*

"*Why?*" *Cyrus asked, "It will make her situation worse because she will confront the king and he will make her a captive in the palace. She will no longer be able to tell him no, or stop him. She also has no way of turning the girls back to normal. We keep going and when we get out of here we can look for some way to fix the situation.*"

With nods all around, the men shuffled out of the room. James followed Cyrus, but as he was about to turn down the hallway when he thought he saw a rock move out of the corner of his eye. He turned to look, but the rock was not moving. Shaking his head, James caught up with Cyrus.

They continued down the hallway. Nothing suspicious was seen or heard as they went. It was like this dungeon was abandoned. James might have believed it, except he still remembered the sounds he heard while they were waiting for everyone else to wake up. There was something out there, but they might not be able to hear it over the noise of they were making. None of the men were worried about disturbing whatever lived there, so they did nothing to muffle their footfalls.

James felt his anxiety increase as they went further along the hallway. He kept thinking he was seeing the rocks lying on the floor move, but any time he looked directly at it there was nothing. James wondered if it was lack of sleep or just the creepiness of the dungeon getting to him. Cyrus pushed on without appearing to notice anything strange. The men muttered to each other, but otherwise focused forward.

About the same distance between doorways as before another one came into sight. This was also a circular room with a statue. This statue was similar in dress as the first one, but her hair was pulled back out of her face by a gold hair clip that had not changed to stone. Her features were closer to her mother's than her father's features. Cyrus stopped only briefly to examine the princess before continuing down the hallway.

There did not seem to be anything else but at regular intervals doorways with circular rooms where a princess stood waiting to be rescued from their stone prison cells. James continued to see rocks move out of the corner of his eye, however no one else seemed to have the same problem. They went past twelve rooms with princesses in them, but the thirteenth room was empty.

"Where is the thirteenth princess?" one of the men asked.

"She probably figured out what happened to her sisters and disappeared her own way," Cyrus answered, "Would not be the first time someone got smart."

About the time another doorway were normally appeared, the group came to an intersection. Cyrus held up his hand, which caused everyone to stop and be quiet. He listened for a minute as he checked both ways. Finally he picked the hallway on the right. Everyone followed him down.

This hallway looked exactly like the previous one, except there were no doorways off it. Instead there were intersections at twice the frequency. Each time they reached an intersection, Cyrus stopped and checked. James was lost by the time they had made several turns. He did not know whether they were moving forward or going back in the direction they had come from. All he knew was they had not gone back over ground they had covered previously.

Through here James could still see the rocks move in his peripheral vision, but since they had not done anything so far he ignored it. He was not sure if they were a danger to the group, or merely watching them for some other purpose. If the rocks were going to attack, it might be easy to fend them off because they were not really big. James really did not know what it would take though as he had never fought any sort of rock creatures.

After a while, the group stopped to rest. James looked behind them and saw a lot more rocks in the hallway than had been there when they walked through it. The rocks must be following them. No one had anything to eat, so the group moved on after only a few minutes. James checked on the rocks before he started following Cyrus again, but they appeared to be regular stationary rocks.

Cyrus led the group in what felt like further into the maze, but James was not completely sure about whether they were closer to the beginning or the ending. With only torch light they could have been walking a couple hours or days, though days seemed unlikely.

The next intersection, Cyrus stopped the group, James could hear the sound of cloth sliding over the floor. It was coming from the left, which was clean of rocks and sand. Cyrus hesitated an extra few second before turning to the left. James felt a chill as they went down the hallway, because the sound reminded him of the same sound he heard back in the room where they had entered the dungeon. But the lack of rocks made him feel a little better. This hallway was the same as all other hallways down here, though there were no doorways off it.

This hallway went for a lot longer than any of the hallways and they never came across any intersections; though every three point five meters there was a diamond shape scratched into the stone wall. The sound stopped as they went and James listened for any other sounds, but none came. However, James did notice that there was a sound he had been hearing which he was not any more. Since leaving that first room there had been a low level rumbling, which he had not really noticed until now that he could not hear it. James wondered if it had been connected to the rocks they had left behind at the intersection.

Finally they reached the end of the hallway, and rather than an intersection or doorway, was a door with handle and a knocker. It was made from wood and painted bright red; a cheery looking door in a dark dungeon in the basement of a palace. The door went right across the hallway, so there was no cheery house for it to go in despite the fact that it looked like it should go in one.

Cyrus stepped forward, but James and the rest of the group stayed back. He used the knocker and tapped lightly three times. James found himself holding his breath and let it out slowly. As he started to monitor his breathing, the door opened. In the doorway stood an old woman. She was about five feet and was skinny enough James was not sure he could not see her bones through her skin. Her white hair stuck up in all directions. She wore a grey skirt and a formerly white blouse, both of which barely stayed on her as they were too big and looked ancient. Her blue eyes were cloudy, but her face otherwise looked like any other old woman.

"I have been waiting for you," she creaked, "Come in." She stepped to one side to let everyone pass.

No one said anything as they shuffled in. The room they entered matched the door. It was cheery with yellow curtains on what should have been windows, but were merely paintings which glowed. The walls were either painted to look like wood painted red, or were red wood put on the stone walls. There was a table in the midst of the room with twelve chairs set around it. Along the right wall was a fire place and work area for cooking. On the wall across from the door was another doorway, which had a curtain across it, but it was likely to be a bedroom.

James sat down on the seat next to Cyrus and tried not to look nervous. The rest of the men seated themselves, leaving the chair closest to the fire for the old woman. She closed the door before going to the fire where a kettle was boiling. On the table were twelve tea cups of various styles, along with a plate of cookies. The woman used a towel to take the kettle off its hook and take it to the table. She poured water into the tea pot before putting the kettle back. After putting the lid on the tea pot, she poured some in each cup. The tea pot never ran out of water as she poured, but there was plenty for each cup. Finally she handed out the cups along with a cookie to each man and James. Then she took her own cup and cookie before sitting down.

"I suppose you have some questions for me," she said before

taking a sip of tea.

"Who are you?" Cyrus asked.

"Lady Walsh," the old woman answered, "My son currently sits on the throne."

"Are you the one who cursed him?" Cyrus asked.

"I did," Lady Walsh answered, "He angered me, so I told him he would be without a son unless he gave up his long life. He refuses to do such and to taunt me he puts the statues of his daughters down here in the dungeon, where he put me shortly after he was crowned. I have been living down here since."

"What else is down here?" Cyrus asked, "Aside from rock creatures."

"The rock creatures are here to keep people in line," Lady Walsh answered, "The travelers are sucked dry by the shadow. The rock creatures will not attack you unless you attack them first."

"How do we get passed the shadow?" Cyrus asked.

"You give it something it cannot eat," Lady Walsh answered. The men looked at each other in confusion, even James was trying to figure out what a shadow does not eat.

"What did you all do to anger my son?" Lady Walsh asked.

"We are on a mission that will remove the Steward from power," Cyrus answered, "The Steward asked King Tezacoati to get rid of us in exchange for removing the curse."

"A foolish child my son always was," Lady Walsh said, "Nothing anyone can do will remove that curse. I may not be powerful in many ways, but curses I know well. For instance, I know you wear one yourself and it tires you."

"It is meant to tire me," Cyrus answered, "But I need no instructions as I know how to rid myself of it if I come across the right circumstance."

"Well, rest up," Lady Walsh said, "You will need your strength for what is to come." She smiled with a motherly way. James felt safe in this cottage, but he wondered about the rest of the people sent down here by King Tezacoati. If she gave them the same

information as she had given this group, why did none of them survive? Surely if someone had survived it would be known that Lady Walsh was down there and no one would be worried about being put down here, which the city folks definitely were. Also the shadow was still haunting the dungeon. Or maybe she gave them the same information and they could not solve the riddle of what a shadow cannot eat.

Once they were all finished the tea and cookies, Lady Walsh ushered the group out her door. She wished them well and said she hoped they survived to help out her daughter-in-law. Cyrus turned to ask how she knew, but she had already closed the door. Rather than say anything to the cheery door, Cyrus turned back and took the lead as they headed back down the hallway.

James tried to stay close to Cyrus, but occasionally found himself falling behind as he tried to think of something a shadow could not eat. Once he bumped into the man behind him, which resulted in grumbling. After that he tried to keep enough of his mind on his speed to keep up with Cyrus. A shadow sucks the life out of anything with life, so humans, animals, elves, dwarfs, dragons, fairies, enchanted objects, and plants. Inanimate objects could disintegrate in the face of such a being. James's mind went over and over this riddle.

The group got back to the intersection. The rocks were all sitting as if the roof had tried to collapse in this area, except there was no damage to the ceiling or walls. Cyrus, James, and the men were careful about stepping around the rocks as they went straight to the next hallway. The hallway was back to having regular intersections, at which Cyrus once again was back to stopping and checking before deciding which way to go. James followed Cyrus, but his mind kept working on the riddle.

Several hours went by. The group stopped once to rest and then continued. Everyone missed their bags and the supplies in them. The tea and cookie given to them by Lady Walsh had barely touched their hunger, which was now back with vengeance. A few rumbling stomachs forced the group to get up and move on. Cyrus must have been letting his own stomach get to him because at least twice he picked the wrong turn and they had to go back to an intersection after hitting a dead end.

James barely noticed as he was busy in his own head. His hunger pains were not as bad because he was too busy to notice. He did, however, manage to keep close to Cyrus and out of the way of the other men.

Finally the group stumbled into a room which was large, square with a closed door on the other side. All around the room were piles of bones and cloth from previous travelers, who had succumb to the shadow. The group pulled out their weapons, but James left his sheathed because he did not think it would do any good to the shadow. The group moved forward carefully and on full alert, until the sound of rocks shifting against each other came from behind them. The group turned around to find the rocks that had been following them were building a wall in the doorway they had just come through. Now there was no way out, except the door on the other side. A couple men went toward that door. They did not reach it because the shadow appeared in front of the door before they could reach it. As soon as they saw the shadow, the men stopped and backed up to the group.

The shadow gave a high pitched cackle. Then it swooped at the group. Those who did not duck, scattered. James had ducked with Cyrus. His mind was back on the situation, but still working on what a shadow could not eat. With the second swoop from the group, one of the men tried to swing his sword at the shadow. The sword went right through, throwing him off balance and doing nothing to the shadow. James skittered away from where the shadow was swooping down on the men, who were trying to figure out what to do about getting rid of the shadow. So far everyone had avoided the shadow, but that was not likely to last.

James looked around the room. The shadow obviously did not eat bones, cloth, or metal, but those could not be fed to the shadow *as they would pass right through. The walls were also useless as they do not keep the shadow in place. Nothing any of the group had with them was likely to be something the shadow could not eat. James's eyes stopped at the wall where the doorway used to be. Would the shadow just suck the life out of the rocks, making them just rocks? Most enchanted objects were intelligent, but the rocks lacked any thoughts of their own, they knew only their purpose. The rocks probably just followed the orders from the shadow.*

And idea came to James. He moved to the wall of rocks before turning toward the shadow. The shadow was just coming out a swoop at the men, who were scattering again. It turned and went again. The men got out of the way, except James. The shadow continued on towards James. Cyrus was on his feet trying to get to James before the shadow did, but he was too far away. As the shadow was just about to hit him, James jumped out of the way. He could have sworn that the shadow brushed passed him. It hit the wall of rocks that had been behind James just a second ago. There was a shriek of horror as the shadow collided with the rocks. Then both disappeared.

Everyone froze as they waited to see if the shadow returned. It did not after five minutes, so they felt safe to move. The men congratulated James on his quick thinking and all anger at his presence seemed to be gone. James accepted it. Finally everyone was ready to go. Cyrus opened the door and stepped through it. James and the rest followed him. The other side of the door was a cave with an opening about ten feet in front of them. Outside the cave was the forest on the other side of the city, with the wall being a distance behind them while front of them was more forest.

The sun was high above them, making it about noon. The forest was peaceful and calm. A few men looked around and found some berries and roots which were edible. So, the group sat down under a tree and ate what had been gathered for lunch. When they were done, Cyrus led them further into the forest.

It was getting close to supper time when they came across a village. Cyrus and two others went into the village to gather news and supplies. They were there only a short time before coming back with what was needed. The bags were filled with everything would need to continue their journey and there was no news from the capital. King Tezacoati had either not found out they had escape, or he was not bothering to search for them. Either way, they figured it was best to leave the country to continue their quest. Since Cyrus had not been keeping the map in his bag, but in his pocket, they still had it. He studied it for a few moments before starting to lead the group the same direction they had been going since leaving the dungeon. They went around the village before really focusing on following the course the map set out for them.

Arabella quit reading and was going to lay the book aside when Waldemar sat up. He was so engrossed in the story, he had not fallen asleep as he usually did. Now he wanted to know what was going to happen next to James.

"Please can you read one more chapter," Waldemar asked. Arabella looked at him and for a moment, he was sure she would tell him to go to sleep.

"All right," Arabella said, "But only one more, then you have to go to sleep."

"I will," Waldemar replied.

"It took them three days before they left the forest behind," Arabella said.

Aside from the usual creatures, they saw very little in the forest and nothing that worried them. Also what they could get for news suggested that King Tezacoati had not figured out that they were gone. There was also no word from Kendrick, but Cyrus said that it was not a surprise for Kendrick to be too busy to send any messages about where he was and when he would be back. That left James disappointed, but the men were more welcoming for the first couple days. They did not turn to him, but ignored him less. None spoke of getting rid of him anymore. However, to be fully part of the group, he was going to have to be helpful a lot more during this adventure. Cyrus treated James the same as he had always treated him. James appreciated Cyrus more for that than the rest for their shifting opinions.

There was not much on the other side of the forest, which ended at the roots of the mountain. The first few mountains were not very big, but standing at the base they still looked pretty big. Since the group had rested not long before they reached the edge of the trees, Cyrus did not stop to sight see. He just headed up the grassy slope. The rest of the group followed him. James took half a moment to stare up the mountain before catching up to the group.

The grass went half way up the mountain and after that it was rocks. A narrow path existed between the boulders. It was a fairly easy hike aside from the steepness. And if they turned to look, they were starting to get above the trees, so the view was no longer blocked. A little farther up and the treetops were completely out of the way. The group stopped about there and everyone found a boulder to sit on while they had a bite to eat. James stared out at the view as he ate.

The trees went on forever with a few places that looked like mere clearings, but were villages and towns. Even the capital was visible from there with the palace spiraling upwards from the midst of the city. Some of the smaller buildings were visible as the space between the trees was much bigger there. James wondered if someone sitting in the window at the top of the spiral could see them sitting there on the mountain. It seemed unlikely due to the group wearing colours that blended into the boulders and dirt behind them.

It was not long before Cyrus got the group moving. James wondered briefly about this, but then overheard someone mutter something about trolls being plentiful in these mountains. One never rests long if there is a chance to encounter a troll, as they were nasty beasts with bad tempers, smelled horrid, and were not easily defeated. The last time the trolls came down out of the mountains and caused damage it took a group of wizards to come along and send them back. Since then the trolls have stayed in the mountains, but if one did not have to one did not venture into their territory, or did so very carefully. Staying still meant they were likely to be smelled out and have to face the consequences. Moving they had a better chance of getting through unnoticed. However, James thought it strange to keep moving on the first mountain side as trolls were less likely to frequent it. But Cyrus was the leader and he seemed to know what he was doing.

The path got narrower and the boulders got closer together. Dirt was becoming thinner and less of it was seen. The slope got steeper and James knew they were getting closer to the top of the mountain. Soon they were climbing more than walking. James had spent the last while getting used to walking and climbing was much more tiring, however he did not dare fall behind or ask for help. He was careful to climb behind and to the right of Cyrus so as not to be hit with any rocks Cyrus dislodged in his climb.

The sky was getting dark when the group reached a plateau at the top of the mountain. The view from up there was even better than the one below because now James could see farther out and lights were coming on in the villages and the capital. He turned to look at what was ahead of them and found it to be bigger mountains. There were plenty of them too. It was going to be a long walk to get through them and he was tired from getting up this first one. The next one was going to be harder. James sat and enjoyed the rest and the food, because he knew Cyrus was not going let them rest here tonight. He was not sure Cyrus was going let them sleep until they were passed the mountains, but James would figure out what to do about that later when he was about to collapse from exhaustion.

As expected, Cyrus had the group up and moving after about half an hour. James got up with the group, dusted himself off, and followed Cyrus over the edge. This edge was much steeper and James was left searching for hand and foot holds. The sun was setting on the other side of the mountain, so he was forced to search by feel.

Fortunately there seemed to be plenty for him to use. James went slowly, but he made progress. The men above him did the same. He was not sure how far Cyrus was below him because he could neither hear nor see him.

James was not sure how long it would be this steep, but he was tiring and becoming unsure of his hand holds. It seemed to be only by luck that he did not slip. Then he came to an area, where he could not find any hand holds. He had been moving so fast that he did not realize he was out of holds until neither foot had one. James found his hands slipping from their holds. He closed his eyes as he felt his hands, which were already slippery with sweat and aching with tiredness, let go. But before he slid very far, someone grabbed him at the waist and set him down on a rock ledge. He opened his eyes and in what little light was left, he saw that Cyrus had been the one to grab him and the ledge was actually a path which headed down the rest of the mountain at a much slower incline. It was back to a narrow path between boulders, which cheered James up because it would be much easier going.

The rest of the men reached the area and everyone rested for a moment. Cyrus took out a pin, which looked like a lily, and pinned it on to his cloak. He rubbed it once and the lily started to glow. It was not a bright light, but it was enough for James to see him. When he set off along the path between the boulders, James was grateful for it because now he could see where Cyrus was, making him easy to follow.

Cyrus went a little slower and the men were much quieter as they traveled. James followed their example because now they were definitely in troll country. Trolls did not have the most acute hearing, but their hearing was good and they could smell people and animals at a distance.

James was so busy following Cyrus's light that he almost did not notice the glow coming from farther in front of them until he could no longer see Cyrus's light because the other was too bright. Cyrus was going into a crouch as he got closer and James followed his example. The rest of the men did likewise. As they got closer, James could smell what could only be described as troll, though he had never before encounter them. The smell was like cabbage that had sat out in the sun too long and then was rolled into a worst smelling bog and then let bake in the sun some more all the time while turning into compost.

Cyrus stopped behind a boulder and everyone else joined him. They looked over the boulder down at the light. It was a camp fire with five grey skinned creatures that had hair growing out of places hair normally did not grow. Their faces lacked symmetry and they wore a piece of cloth over what James assumed was breeding equipment but nothing else. They were eating some mountain goats, which they had roasted over the fire. They were sloppy with their food and drink. Instead of talking they grunted at each other.

Someone quietly asked Cyrus if the group was up wind of the trolls or down wind. Cyrus responded in the same volume that he did not know because he could not feel any wind. Finally Cyrus must have felt he had seen enough as he signaled for everyone to get behind the boulder. James was more than happy to stop looking at the ugly creatures. Cyrus started back up the mountain and the group followed. When there was space between some boulders he turned to the left and followed that narrow path for a while. When it turned back down toward the trolls' camp, he went back towards the mountain again.

Slowly they made their way around the trolls' camp in the zigzag manner of following the narrow paths. When they were on the other side of the camp, Cyrus stopped for a moment to let the men rest. James looked back the way they had come and saw they were exactly opposite from where they had last observed the camp. The trolls were finishing up the goats and looked like they were thinking of getting some sleep. James was relieved until he saw one of the trolls take several sniffs of the air. James pulled back to where Cyrus was sitting.

"I think we are down wind," James whispered. Cyrus pulled

himself up for a look.

"I think you are right," Cyrus whispered back before signaling the men up the mountain. They continued to crouch, but they started moving. James did the same and Cyrus followed him. There were not many places to go because the boulders kept the group going along three narrow paths that were parallel to each other.

There was a roar from the camp below. James's first instinct was to look, but his second was to hurry up. He followed his second, so he did not see the trolls charging in their direction. Cyrus started pushing James into a run and he quickly took it up. The smell from the trolls was getting stronger.

"We have to out climb the trolls," Cyrus's voice was close to James. James nodded, but could do nothing else in response except run faster. The rest of the men must have already known this as they quit crouching and just headed up into the mountain at a full run. James thought about standing, but Cyrus pulled him down and pushed him forward.

The boulders went on for a while before the ground became steeper and the path disappeared. James was running as fast as he could, but he was getting tired and the trolls seemed to have decided they were enjoying the exercise. He was starting to think it was impossible to out run a troll when he ran into a flat stone. James hit hard enough to give his head something to wonder about, but he did not have any time to recover before Cyrus had him up and was pushing him to climb the rock. James scrambled for foot and hand holds, which once he found the first ones it was easier to find the next ones. His head was still spinning a little bit, but any time he paused Cyrus would prod him to keep climbing.

The trolls reached the bottom of the rock, but found little for them to climb on and the hand holds were much too small for them to get any grip. Instead they started to throw their clubs at Cyrus and James. James was reaching out for the next hand hold when a club flew up and hit the rock above him. He turned his head away from the shower of rocks and pulled himself as close to the cliff as he could to avoid the falling club. As soon as it was clear, he tried to speed up. It was difficult with finding hand holds without light, Cyrus close behind, his tiredness, and the trolls clubs hit the wall all around James although none getting as close as the first one.

Several minutes went by before James and Cyrus were too far up for the trolls to throw their clubs. The trolls stood there for several minutes before James could hear them walk away. James hoped it was to go back to their camp and not to find another way up the cliff. Then James had to focus on climbing because he missed a hand hold and slipped, but caught himself before he hit Cyrus. Cyrus stopped and let him get his gripe back instead of prodding him to keep going.

Finally James reached up to grab the next hand hold and found the edge of the cliff. He pulled himself up and rolled away from the edge as he felt too tired to get to his feet. Based on the murmur of voices several of the men from the rest of group were already there. Cyrus pulled himself up a moment later. The light from his pin showed seven of the men were sitting there and there were no trolls in sight. The other two men were still working their way up the cliff, so there was no point in doing anything aside from finding somewhere to sit and wait for them.

James peeked over the edge at the fire below. The light from the fire seemed the fill the valley between mountains. The trolls had set up their camp at the very bottom between the mountains. Visible by the light were the five trolls around the fire. They were moving around almost as if they were packing up their camp. James wondered if they were moving to a place where they would not be disturbed, or whether they did not want to leave their camp unattended while they hunted for the men who had entered their domain. He hoped they were just looking for a new camping spot.

The other two men got up on to the ledge, one with an injured leg. They quickly bandaged the wound up before everyone gathering themselves together to keep going. James waited as long as possible before standing. He would have fallen asleep, except that the excitement of getting away from the trolls was keeping him awake. The men started the next part of the climb, while Cyrus waited for James to get moving before following him up.

The group did not reach the top of this mountain, but stopped on a ledge barely big enough for all of them to sit on. Since it would take real work to get on or off the ledge, Cyrus felt it was safe enough for them to stop and rest. James was nestled close to the wall with Cyrus on one side and another man on the other side. He curled up as only a child could and fell asleep.

The sunshine was what woke James up, as it hit him square in the face. He uncurled and stretched being careful of those on either side. Cyrus was already awake, but the man on the other side was waking up same as James. The sun had just come over the horizon and lit up the whole ledge, causing them all to wake up and blink at the bright light.

When they were awake enough, they all had something to eat. Then they got ready for another day of climbing. It was much easier to climb today as now James could see the hand holds. He could also see how far there was to fall, but he focused on the up rather than the down so he would not do anything foolish out of fear or panic. Cyrus stayed behind him to make sure he kept moving and did not slip. However, James was well rested and more than able to keep going on his own.

They rested briefly at noon to eat lunch, but otherwise kept working on getting to the top. James wondered if it was really necessary to go over all the mountains, or whether they really should be just going in between them. But he supposed Cyrus knew where he was going. He had the map after all. The sun shone on the group for the day without a single cloud getting in the way. It provided them with some warmth, which they needed because the air was getting cold and thin. The farther up they went the less there was for ledges they could rest on and it was not because there were less ledges so much as there was snow on the ledges.

Any time snow landed on their clothes or body, it would melt in the sun as they climbed and then they would end up wet, which then would make them cold due to the temperature of the air. So, they avoided the snow as much as they could. But the day was getting on and the sun was getting closer to the horizon. James wondered whether they would try to continue in the dark, or clean off a ledge. They reached a ledge big enough for them all just as the sun was about to disappear. The men cleaned off what they could given the circumstances and accepted what they could not do. Again this ledge was not a place trolls could get to easily, even though they had not seen trolls all day.

The group had supper and then settled in for the night. James was drifting off between Cyrus and another man from the group feeling achy and cold. He had a brief thought about his bed back at the farm, where it would not be as cold, but the other issues made him okay with sleeping on a mountain in the cold, snow, and wind. James felt a finger tap his shoulder and opened his eyes. Cyrus had a finger to his lips so that James would not say anything and then he pointed up the mountain face. None of the other men were awake. James uncurled himself enough to start climbing and Cyrus followed behind him.

They went up for a long while and James was starting to wonder why they were leaving the others behind when he reached a ledge he had not noticed despite searching for anything above him. He climbed up on top and found himself in a cave rather than on a ledge in the wind. It was not a very big cave, so it would make sense not to bring the whole group, or to try and sleep here. Cyrus climbed to stand beside James.

"Why are we here?" James asked.

"Before we get the jewel, we need the key," Cyrus answered, "And the key is here." James turned back toward the cave, but did not see anything that looked like a key.

"Where is this key?" James asked.

"In here," Cyrus answered as he pushed on a piece of rock and

a small opening appeared at the base of the wall. Cyrus could not have fit into the opening if he was naked and greased, but James could fit with a little extra room to spare.

"I do not know what specifically guards it," Cyrus said, "But it should not be anything you cannot handle on your own." James looked at the opening for half a moment before preparing himself.

"I will try," James said before crawling inside. The tunnel was dark and about twenty feet long. James could not hear, or smell anything at the other end, but his mind was worried about trolls. This was their territory and he was sure they preferred caves when they were up this high in the mountains.

James finally reached the end of the tunnel and found himself in a larger space with a light coming from somewhere to his right. He followed it and stopped in front of a key handing on a peg in the rock wall with a light shining down from somewhere unseen. There was no creatures around that James could see, or any visible defenders of it.

Hesitantly James reached up to take the key down. Nothing happened. So James closed his fingers around the key. There was a burst of light which caused James to be thrown back against the wall. He had closed his eyes against the light as he was thrown backward, but once he was stopped moving and lay crumpled at the bottom of the wall he opened them back up again. He was still holding on to the key. Standing in front of him was an old looking man in a flowing deep, blue robe, but the man looked almost ghost-like in that James could see through him.

"I am the guardian of this key," the man's voice echoed in the small chamber, "You have to have proved your worth to have taken such a prize. Use it for good in the world and protect it from the evil of the world." The man finished speaking and flickered once before disappearing. He left the room dark and it took James several minutes before he could make anything out.

Finally light from the tunnel was visible, though very faint. James tucked the key into his pocket and crawled toward the tunnel.

He crawled through it and back out to the cave where Cyrus was waiting. James collapsed again. He felt like a whole lot of power had gone through him when the burst of light had appeared and now his muscles were fatigued. Cyrus checked his pulse and when he found one, he left James alone to recover on his own. James could feel his heart hammering away in his chest and there was a slight tingling in his fingers and toes.

Lying there in the cold helped James feel somewhat better. After a few minutes he was able to sit up and lean against the wall.

"What happened?" Cyrus asked offering James his water skin. James took a drink before handing it back to Cyrus.

"I got the key, but there was some kind of spell on it," James answered, "And an apparition showed up and called itself the guardian. It said I was allowed to take the key because I had been proven worthy, but I should protect it from evil."

"Rest now," Cyrus said, "When you are ready we will go back down to the group. Tomorrow we can go around to the other side of the mountain and head down."

"Then we will be out of the mountains?" James asked.

"No," Cyrus answered, "We will not being going through the whole range, but our next stop in the Darkened Valley, which is still a couple mountains away. We just turn west rather than continue north. It will take another day or two to get through the mountains."

James nodded, but he felt too tired to ask any more questions despite the large number of them going through his head. He was going to ask if Cyrus wanted the key, but he forgot with all the talk of going over mountains. Cyrus let him sit and collect himself. They had all night to get back down to the rest of the group. Though James did not want to stay up here all night because he would get very little sleep that way and he needed the sleep.

When he was sure he could stand without collapsing, James got to his feet. He went to the edge and Cyrus helped him down before following him down. James was able to find the ledge the rest of the group was on without difficulty, but exhaustion had taken hold on his way down and he was only barely able to get down without slipping. Once on the ledge, he collapsed and was not able to get back up. Cyrus sat down next to him and leaned against the cliff wall. James did not remember closing his eyes, but the night took him away in the form of sleep and the world no longer mattered anymore.

The sun once again woke James up as it came over the horizon, but James did not move at all. The light burned at his eye lids, but he did not open them. He could hear the groans of those around him waking to the sun's light. People began to move as they sat up and stretched. James wanted to go back to sleep, but he felt he should get up so as not to slow down the group. James willed his eyes to open, but they did not move. He tried to move his hands, but they stayed where they were. James felt a hand on his neck checking his pulse. He was sure that there was one to be found.

"Is he all right?" one of the men asked. It sounded like he was the man on the opposite side of James from Cyrus.

"He is alive," Cyrus answered, "But he seems to be unable to move. Likely the cause is too much exercise in too thin air."

"We have been doing the same with no ill effects," one of the other men said.

"But we are not the same age or physical condition as the boy," someone else replied, "He barely made it up here yesterday. The only cure for him is to let him rest until he gets over the exhaustion."

"We cannot afford to let him slow us down," the man said.

"If you wish to rush off, would you be willing to carry him?" Cyrus asked. There was muttering from the man, but no agreement from him. No one else spoke up. James felt a cloak being laid down over him and part of it fell across his eyes which blocked out the sun. James accepted the consensus to let him sleep.

James regained consciousness when the sun shined over the edge *of the cloak. It must have been noon as the sun was at its height in the sky. No one around him was talking, but it sounded like they were eating. James tried to open his eyes and found they were willing to do so this time. He could see the cloak but not much else. The fingers on his right hand twitched without him thinking about it. In fact he had several muscles which were twitching, but none were preventing him from moving.*

Cautiously James sat up. Everything seemed to be working and he was not as tired as he was before. Cyrus offered him something to eat, which James accepted. They all ate without talking. When they were finished, everyone packed up. James gave the cloak back and was otherwise ready to go. Cyrus merely picked up his bag and was ready. A few of the others had to repack their bags, but they did so quite quickly.

It was only two minutes before Cyrus led the way along the rock face to head around the mountain instead of heading closer to the top. James was close behind him with everyone else coming along as well. When they got around to the other side, Cyrus got the group headed down the mountain. It was much darker because the sun was on the other side of the mountain, but there was still enough light to see. As the sun was not there to melt it, there was plenty of snow on the ledges, ridges, and any other flat areas. This made it a little tricky to keep climbing. One of the men dropped several feet because he slipped. However, he did manage to catch himself before he hit something that could have injured him.

The group was getting close to the next section of the mountain when there was a shriek that echoed off the mountains and caused them all to stop and look around. There was nothing in sight, but it definitely sounded like there was something alive in these mountains. Cyrus started moving again and James, along with everyone else, did the same.

When the group did reach the boulders, Cyrus was careful as he came down from the wall. Not seeing anything that was a danger, he signaled for the rest to come down as well. They moved along the narrow path between the boulders. Cyrus kept watching for any trolls, but he saw none. The group walked across the valley between the mountains. No trolls showed themselves and nothing else came at the group. At one time, James thought he saw a white hairy creature high up near the snow line of the mountain they were headed towards, but he blinked and it disappeared so he was not really sure if he had seen it or whether it was his mind playing tricks on him.

The valley was far across and the sun disappeared completely, leaving only a trace of light for a very short time. Cyrus rubbed his pin and again it gave them enough light to see him. However, with the darkness everyone stayed close together in case there were trolls out there that they could not see until ambushed by them.

When they reached the end of the boulders and thus the end of the valley, the moon came out to show them the snow covered ground that was next. There were no cliff faces to climb or ledges to sleep on, just snow to wade. Cyrus kept going. The rest followed as no one wanted to stop anywhere as they could still remember the shriek. Until they found a safe place, they did not want to stop to rest.

If was not long before all of them had feet that were soaked from the snow. The wind picked up as well, which made them all wrap their cloaks closer to them. Cyrus followed a track, which led up into the mountain. James had seen from the valley that going up the mountain was the only way to get out of the valley and they could not have gone around it get where they wanted to go.

About the time the sun should have been coming out, it started to snow. The blizzard gathered around the group as if something was not happy with their presence on the mountain. The group pushed on anyway. They were quickly soaked from the snow and freezing from the wind. The sun itself brightened the sky, but stayed behind the clouds. The wind got sharper as they went farther up the mountain. Along with having walked through the night, the group was starting to get tired. James himself had gone from feeling well rested to wandering how he was able to continue to put one foot in *front of the other. Cyrus never slowed down or stopped, but he could tell that the rest of the group were going to need to rest soon.*

As they went, Cyrus saw a cave opening farther up the mountain and headed towards it. No one complained, or worried about the trolls. When they reached the cave, everyone stayed outside while Cyrus went inside to check the cave for any inhabitants. He did not find any trace of something living there, so he signaled for the rest of the group to enter. As much as they wanted a fire to thaw out, no one dared light one. Instead they ate a cold supper and wrapped themselves in their bedrolls. James lay near where Cyrus sat and tried not to let his teeth chattering stop him from sleeping.

James was starting to drift off when he heard something, which was not a sound he recognized as being from any member in the group. He started to sit up, but Cyrus stopped him by laying a hand on his shoulder. James laid back down and listened. Something at the back of the cave was making the noise. There was a thumping and a slight squeaking.

Cyrus had silently slipped his sword out and set it across his lap. James knew he could not get at either of his weapons without making noise, so he stayed still. No one else were moving, though it could have been that James could not see them and they were being silent to hear the sounds coming from the back of the cave. It sounded a bit like something was trying to get through the back of the cave and get into the cave itself.

There was a groan, or grunt, which did not match the noises so far. Cyrus let James get up. James moved close enough so Cyrus would not have to speak too loudly.

"Get a fire going," Cyrus whispered, "Use the wood in the bag." Cyrus pushed his bag closer to James. James got to his feet and picked up the bag. He took it to the middle of the group which was clear. Using the wood from the bag and a handful of leaves, which were in the bottom of the bag. He set it out and used his flint and steel to make some sparks. It took a short amount of time before the leaves were burning. The wood took a little longer to catch

on fire. It started out bright, but eventually filled the cave with light.

No one could see what was happening, but they could definitely hear it. James could now see that everyone was awake and sitting up. Their weapons gleamed in the fire light. James took out his dagger before going back to where Cyrus was sitting.

There was a loud bang and the wall at the back of the cave came crashing down. A group of trolls charged in. They were a different from the trolls they had seen before, but that did not make them any less dangerous. Cyrus and the rest of the men jumped up to attack. James did not move from where he was, but he did change from sitting to squatting. James noticed Cyrus stayed near the fire, but the trolls did not seem to be affected by the light. The men closest to the trolls attacked first, but swords were not very useful as the trolls healed much too quickly. The cuts were not enough and not quick enough to take the trolls down. When a troll got close to Cyrus, he did not swing his sword, but instead he reached down and grabbed a branch from the fire. The troll's hair caught on fire as did its cloth piece. The troll started to cry out as Cyrus kept the burning branch close to the troll as its skin started to blacken.

Two of the men near the new hole in the cave got on either side of a troll and managed to keep it distracted as one took his sword to the troll's neck. He got his sword through the skin and all the way through the neck. The head rolled away and the body slumped down to the ground. But more trolls were pouring through the hole and the men were having trouble doing enough damage to deal with the trolls.

The troll that Cyrus was burning caught fully on fire and dropped in an effort to put itself out. But the flames lapped up something on the troll and continued to burn it. Cyrus kicked the troll into another one, which knocked the other troll on top of the one that was burning. That one found himself catching on fire as well. Both of them tried to put out the flames, but were not very successful. The next troll thought about attacking Cyrus briefly, but after looking at the burning branch Cyrus was still holding in his hand, moved on to attack someone else.

The trolls left James alone because he was not the biggest threat in the room, but he feared that with more trolls pouring in, that they would notice him and attack him as well. Cyrus used the burning branch on a troll that appeared to be headed toward James, but James did not think Cyrus could hold them all off. At this point, every man was fighting one or more trolls and were not being as successful at it as Cyrus was with his branch. One other man had grabbed a branch, but it had been knocked out of his hand before he could light any of the trolls on fire. The branch lay on the floor and looked like it might make a troll burn anyway, but then it was stamped out.

Suddenly there was a high and sharp cry, which stretched into a howl. None of the trolls made the sound and everyone turned toward the cave entrance where the sound had come from. Standing there was the white, hairy creature James had thought he had seen earlier. It beat its hands against its chest as it continued to howl. The trolls screeched and rushed back toward the hole in the back of the cave. They were pushing each other out of the way and trampled anything in their way. The men hurried to get out of the way. When they were all through, the trolls put some big rocks in the hole to close it up.

When James saw that the trolls were gone, he turned back to the entrance. The creature was gone. Cyrus picked up the burning branch that was on the floor before putting both branches into the fire. The rest of the men made sure everyone was okay before settling back on their bedrolls. James moved closer to the fire, which was built bigger using wood pieces others had brought with them. Everyone crowded near the fire to finish thawing out and drying out. No one said anything as they sat there, but James kept glancing from the back of the cave to the entrance.

"Neither are going to bother us for the rest of the night," Cyrus finally told him.

"What was that?" James asked looking at the entrance again. There was nothing there and it was like nothing had ever been there.

"No one is sure what it calls itself," Cyrus answered, "But it helps some and attacks others without any apparent reasons why. Trolls and other beasts fear it. Once it scares them off, they did not come back for a long time, so we are safe here for the night."

James nodded as again he had more questions, but was getting sleepy from the long walk and then the attack. He curled up within the warmth of the fire and let the crackle of flames lull him to sleep.

In the morning the fire had died and only embers remained. There was not even enough warmth to heat up breakfast. Instead everyone ate their food cold as they had so far during this adventure and packed up. They got ready to leave the cave.

Outside the snow had stopped falling and the wind had calmed a small amount. Cyrus set a fast pace, but no one was going to complain. The sooner they got out of the mountains the better. They continued up the snow covered slope. James thought at one point he had seen the creature again, but then when he looked again it was just dirty snow.

Cyrus led them up to the area where the rock got steeper and there was less snow accumulation, but instead of climbing it Cyrus led the group on a path around it. They walked around it until they came to the other side of the mountain. From there it was straight down the mountain and into the Darkened Valley. James was surprised that there was no more mountains to climb over, but glad at the sight of flat ground. The men around him started to murmur about the woods, which were at the bottom of the slope. However, it was only when they rested while eating lunch did James listen to what they were saying. With relief the men were headed down the mountain, but with trepidation they headed into the Darkened Valley. Very few people came out of the Darkened Valley and those who did rarely were willing to tell the tale. This chilled James through, but he knew Cyrus would not take them into any place the map did not require them to visit.

It took the rest of the day to get to the bottom of the slope. There was a section of grass between the mountain and the woods. Cyrus stopped on the grass and everyone was happy to stop with him. Everyone settled in for the night and Cyrus definitely was not going any further. James found himself a small area, which he hoped would be in the sun in the morning. The coldness of the mountains had not left him yet and he really hoped that being in the sun would get rid of the rest of it, because he figured he would need all the warmth he could get before going into the Darkened Valley.

Supper was passed around as the men also worked to finish warming themselves up. Then finally James wrapped himself up and laid down. He did not close his eyes immediately as he stayed still and listened to the men. There were various conversations happening. Back at the farm, it would have been quiet at this time of night with only the sounds of nature which came into the house. His step-father was always in bed as early as possible and expected the same of James. After all, James needed to be taught how to be a farmer and his step-father was sure he knew exactly how to do it. James was happy to be far away from his step-father and his lessons on how to be a farmer.

Despite being put in a dungeon, frozen in the mountain, and being attack by an evil unicorn, James was much happier on this adventure. He wondered about Kendrick's statement about expecting James to come along. Was James supposed to be on this adventure? If so, who was the one setting all this in motion? And was his leaving the farm his own decision or someone else's?

Waldemar's eyes drifted close. His mother put the book down. She came to the bed and kissed his forehead. His brain acknowledged that he heard the door open and close. Then he went into sleep with visions of adventure going through his mind.

THE SEARCH FOR THE DEMON CONTINUES WHILE THE DEMON FINDS SOME PREY

Weldon had not been sleeping well, so he had gotten up and went to the balcony. He had seen the sun come up and was staring out toward the city gate. Weldon had thought about checking if he could join the search for the demon, but he had not seen anyone awake or looking around. And he was willing to admit that thoughts of joining the search were more to do with the restless feeling he was having. Rana was due back at any time and yet there was no sign of her carriage. With the events happen here at the castle, Weldon worried that someone might also be after her.

The door squeaked open and then closed. Weldon did not turn around but kept his focus on the road up to the castle gate. Out of the corner of his eye, Weldon saw the castle steward stop beside him. The castle steward looked out at the courtyard before turning to Weldon.

"A messenger arrived a few minutes ago," the castle

steward said, "It is from Rana."

"What was the message?" Weldon asked turning to the castle steward.

"The carriage hit a rock and now they are working on fixing the carriage," the castle steward answered, "They are at an inn, so they are not only safe but also comfortable. They will get here as soon as they can get the carriage fixed."

"I guess until then we have to keep searching for the demon on our own," Weldon said.

"The guards have checked the castle over several times," the castle steward said, "We have checked any place where a demon would likely use as a hiding spot. Where else is there to look?"

"I do not know," Weldon said, "That was why I was hoping Rana would arrive today. I guess the other option is to keep an eye on as many as we can. No one should go anywhere alone and we need to try to keep the children supervised."

"I will spread the word," the castle steward said, "And I will ask someone to watch over the children. It will have to be someone closer to their age so that person can keep up with them, as well as the children are not likely to run from them."

"Good," Weldon said, "If we cannot find the demon, we need to protect people who are here."

"I will tell the captain of the guard as well as everyone else I can," the castle steward said. He went back inside. Weldon stayed where he was and continued looking out over the city. He was no longer watching the road, but scanning the city in general. The demon was out there somewhere and they needed to figure out where.

Waldemar opened his eyes and looked around his

room. The curtains had not been closed the night before so the sun was shining in and giving him light. Eldon was nowhere in sight. Waldemar's mother had left the book on the rocking chair before leaving for the night. Everything else was the same as the night before.

Flipping the blanket up, Waldemar got out of bed and went to the wardrobe. He pulled out a different pair of trousers and tugged them on. Waldemar went to the rocking chair and picked up the book. Rather than read it, he stuck it in his pocket and then headed for the door. Waldemar peeked out. There was no one in sight. Waldemar slipped out of his room and headed down the hallway. At each intersection of hallways he stopped and checked, but the way was clear. Waldemar got all the way down the stairs before he had to hide to avoid being seen. It was just the castle steward heading up the stairs, probably on his way to do some sort of duty.

As soon as the castle steward was out of sight, Waldemar continued down the hallway. Damon was sitting outside the kitchen. Waldemar sat down beside his friend.

"We are not allowed to go to the marketplace today," Damon said, "The guards at the gates are watchful and will not allow us out. They are not letting anyone in and court is cancelled."

"What else should we do?" Waldemar asked.

"There has been talk about spending the day in the alcove," Damon said, "But what exactly we are doing, I am not sure."

"I borrowed a book," Waldemar said taking it out of his pocket, "We can read for a while."

"We have to wait until the cook has most of breakfast finished if we want to take any food with us," Damon said, "It should not be too long."

"Okay," Waldemar said as he put the book back into his pocket.

The boys sat there and waited for several minutes. A few of the other children from around the castle joined them. Finally, Damon got up and checked the kitchen. Everyone watched him go into the kitchen and waited for the signal. A moment later, Damon's hand came around the door frame and signalled for the rest to come. Everyone got up and followed him into the kitchen. The food was waiting on the counter as the cook and his assistant were busy somewhere else. The other servants did not bother with the children as each took a little bit of food and went out the door to the courtyard.

Outside the door and to the left was an alcove, which was big enough for the children to gather and relax. There was nothing in there to explain the purpose of the alcove, but no one tried to stop them from gathering there and never had before. There were no guards posted in or near the alcove, even though there were more than normal in the courtyard.

Without much idea of what to do, several games of sticks were started. Waldemar and Damon sat back and watched the closest game as they ate their breakfast. The game of sticks being one of agility and speed the same person usually won, but of the four in the game they were watching were evenly matched game. None of the players were especially good, but none were horrible either.

"So, what is the book?" Damon asked.

"Adventures For a Future King by Thomas Merritt," Waldemar answered.

"What is it about?" Damon asked.

"This boy, who while running away from home, gets recruited to help a group of adventurers search for a jewel," Waldemar answered, "The jewel is supposed to go to the king of this one place to save it from an evil steward."

"So is the main character the future king?" Damon asked.

I do not know yet," Waldemar answered, "I only just finished the third chapter last night and so far they have not mentioned anything about him being a king. They have talked plenty about his life on the farm, but nothing about him being a king. Maybe they meet the future king later in the book and have him join the group, or he somehow gains the throne through some strange happenstance. But I have to finish reading the book to figure it out."

"What happened in chapter three?" Damon asked.

"They went through the mountains," Waldemar answered, "Trolls lived in the mountains and attacked the adventurers, but they were saved by a yeti. The boy found a key that should help them later on in their quest. When Mother stopped last night, the adventurers were just about to enter a place called the Darkened Valley, where no one comes out alive."

"Sounds like fun," Damon said, "Why do you not read the fourth chapter and we will see how they manage to get out alive?"

"Sure," Waldemar replied as he took the book out of his pocket. He opened it up to his Mother's bookmark and started to read.

"The sun did hit spots on the grassy area when it rose the next morning and one of those spots was where James had fallen asleep.

The sun did hit spots on the grassy area when it rose the next morning and one of those spots was where James had fallen asleep. Only this time rather than hitting his face, the sun warmed his back. The warmth made James not want to move, but he instead he stretched and sat up. Everyone else was still asleep as they did not have the sun hitting them to let them know it was morning. The only person awake was Cyrus, who was sitting near the rest of them.

James sat there in the sunny spot and enjoyed the warmth for a little longer, but did not go back to sleep. Eventually the rest of the group started to stir and sit up. Once everyone was awake, breakfast was handed out. James was okay with moving then because the sun had moved on and taken its warmth with it. As soon as breakfast was over, the group got ready and started down the last of the slope.

The farther they went down the slope the darker it became, until they reached the trees and found it almost pitch black. Cyrus used his pin as a light, but it barely gave off enough to see. The men could follow the light, but could not see what was at their feet, which would trip them up. One of them tried to light a torch, but the darkness seemed to surround it and block its usefulness. This made it more difficult to see anything, so the torch was put out and Cyrus's light was the only one left to guide them. James stayed as close to Cyrus as he could since he did not want to get lost.

Even though they could not see them, the group of men could hear the trees around them. The leaves made a rustling noise as the men went passed. There was a slight wind, but it never seemed to reach the men. The usual animals sounds one expected to hear during a walk in the woods were missing. James could hear the noises made by the group, which filled the otherwise empty air. The silence of the woods made everyone in the group uneasy and slightly hesitant. A feeling of dread covered the group and made each feel like they should be running for their lives rather than continuing. However, since everyone else was continuing, they remained where they were.

They had not gone far when Cyrus started to slow down and turn off the straight road he had been following. James grabbed his wrist because he was worried that something had a hold on Cyrus. For a brief moment, James could see a light coming from an ethereal being standing some distance away. She was beautiful with her blonde hair, fair skin, and white flowing dress. The moment was over with before James could see more of the scene and Cyrus was shaking his head. Once he figured out what had happened, Cyrus got back on the straight path he had been following and James let go.

Cyrus was fine after that incident and they continued. James kept watch just in case it happened again. It added another worry to keep James alert along the trees, the silence, and getting lost if they did not stay on the path. Cyrus did not seem to notice any of those worries as he was now focused only on keeping to the path. The rest of the group did not seem worried because Cyrus had not gotten farther off path before coming back to it.

The man behind James started to wander off the path toward a point somewhere off in the distance. James noticed out of the corner of his eyes and reached out. He grabbed the man's wrist. This time James could see two small children playing in the trees, both were oblivious to the danger which was coming up behind them. James had never seen such a creature, but it looked like something out of a nightmare. It huge with sharp teeth, long claws, and white spikes, which was all that could be seen against the darkness. Then it was gone as if it was never there and only darkness was left.

The man stopped and James let go. There was a sound from the man that was almost like a sob. Unlike Cyrus the man was not quite able to shake it off and keep going. He stopped walking and stood there for a minute. It was not until someone asked him if he was all right. Then he seemed to come back to the mission and where they were. The man rejoined the group.

As everyone was back in place, someone at the back of the group was dragged back into the group after they took a couple steps to wander off. That man also took a moment to come back to the present and what was happening. He seemed to have seen something *that horrified him and unsettled him, but he kept going along with the group. James figured if asked, the men would have been willing to go back and find some other way around.*

James's thoughts had started to wonder about what he had seen when a light in the trees caught his eye. He looked toward it and saw someone standing out there. Without thinking about it, James took a step toward it. The figure became more defined and turned into his mother. Behind her was his step-father. He took another step toward them and his step-father's face flickered to something skeletal and non-human. Someone grabbed James's arm and both figures disappeared along with the light. James looked to see that it was Cyrus who was pulling him back to the path. After a slight shake of his head, James went back to the path and continued along it with everyone else.

The men had made a line with a hand on the shoulder of the man in front of him. This would prevent anyone else from wandering off and might stop people from seeing the strange, nightmarish sights. The man at the front took Cyrus's shoulder while Cyrus kept his grip on James's arm. They continued on like this with Cyrus's light being the only way to see anything. James looked ahead, but really could not tell where the path was and whether it was straight or meandered through the trees.

Suddenly there was another light ahead. James wondered if it was just him, but then noticed that Cyrus's grip slackened a little and the whole group slowed down. The light got brighter until it was as tall as the trees and wider than any path. The light showed the dark brown creature clearly. It was a giant spider that looked like it was hungry for supper and the group was his meal. James could even make out the spider's eyes and fangs. To make things worse, instead of the silence they could hear the clicking sounds the spider was making.

Waldemar stopped reading because Damon went stiff beside him and there was a muffled scream from one of the players of the game. He looked up from the book to see a creature like he had never seen before. It was black and white in lines and spots with fingers ending in claws. The human-shaped face was tilted to one side as if it was sniffing the air though there was no nose on its face. There were just black eyes.

Waldemar had never heard of a creature that looked like the one standing there, nor had he read about such a thing, but he was sure it did not have good intentions. He stood up to try and get the group of children under control, but they were too focused on the creature. The guards were too far away to hear shouting or they would already be on their way. Not that Waldemar could see if they were on their way or not, but he had not heard any shouting to indicate they were.

Since he did not have any weapons on him, Waldemar did not know what he could do. Fighting such a being would require some sort of weapon, but none of the rest in the alcove were likely to have anything to fight with either. Waldemar was ready to get everyone screaming for help when he felt tired. He collapsed to the cobblestones as they rest of the children laid down. Waldemar fought to stay awake but did not succeed. His eyes closed, but before he was completely out he thought he felt himself being moved.

The castle steward was taking a brief break to eat some breakfast when the washerwoman's son came and sat down at the table. The castle steward had sent him away half an hour ago to keep an eye on the children. As the washerwoman's son was about thirteen, the castle steward felt he was more likely to be able to watch the children without them complaining about an adult around.

"There is a problem," the washerwoman's son said.

The castle steward thought his name might be Gareth.

"What is the problem?" the castle steward asked.

"The children are gone," Gareth answered.

"The guard were told not to allow them to leave the courtyard," the castle steward said, "Perhaps they are just somewhere other than where you looked."

"They were seen going to the alcove outside the kitchen door," Gareth said, "They took some food with them to have for breakfast. The kitchen staff told me they had been seen. So, I went out there to check on them and there was no one in the alcove."

"They must have gone somewhere else," the castle steward said.

"The guards never saw them leave the alcove," Gareth said, "And there are several unfinished games of sticks lying in the alcove." The castle steward looked up at Gareth thinking to give the boy a sharp tongue lashing, but the boy was honest with him. The children had been in the alcove and were now gone. If they had left their games unfinished they likely did not go willingly and they did not go in such a way as the guards, who were all over the courtyard, did not see them leave.

The castle steward left his breakfast and hurried out of the dining room. Gareth followed him. The castle steward went straight to Weldon's office, where he knew Weldon and the captain of the guard were having a conference on security against demons. Weldon knew a little more about demons than the captain of the guard as he had faced the one who had been manipulating Hillel, but even then Weldon did not know much about this current demon tormenting the castle residents. And it appeared to be only the castle residents as no word of such activities was coming from the city.

The castle steward barely took the time to knock

before entering the officer. Weldon and the captain of the guard were seated at his desk and they both looked up at him.

"What is wrong?" Weldon asked.

"The children have gone missing," the castle steward said, "I sent Gareth here to watch them today and he came back with word that they were gone."

"Are you sure?" the captain of the guard asked Gareth.

"Yes, sir," Gareth answered, "By all accounts they were in the alcove outside the kitchen door and now it looks like they vanished without a trace, except they left their games behind."

"We need to search the castle for any sign of them," the captain of the guard got to his feet.

"Round up any children who were not taken," Weldon said, "And put them under guard somewhere where there are plenty of people around."

"I will, Duke Weldon," the captain of the guards said with a bow before leaving the officer.

"What are we to do?" the castle steward asked.

"Either get Rana back here and hope she can help," Weldon answered, "Or see if we can find this demon ourselves."

"If the captain of the guard is already sending men out to search the castle, there is no point in us doing it again," the castle steward said, "But I will send out another carriage to where we know Rana is stuck. Hopefully, we can get her home faster."

"Good," Weldon said, "Also get everyone gathered in the throne room. Chores and other such can wait until we know more about this demon. In the meantime, we need everyone together to prevent anyone else from going missing."

"I will send out word immediately," the castle steward

said with a bow before leaving. Gareth followed him out.

"What should I do?" Gareth asked once they were in the corridor.

"Go get your mother and gather with everyone else in the throne room," the castle steward answered, "And tell everyone you meet to do the same."

"Yes, sir," Gareth said then hurried off.

The castle steward went off to find a coachman and a carriage to send after Rana.

Arabella had checked Waldemar's room, but once again she found he had left before she had gotten up. The wardrobe still stood open and none of Waldemar's mess had been cleaned up in a couple days, which she thought was strange. The book was also gone, but that did not surprise her. Waldemar really liked this book and had likely taken it with him to read some more of it. She would have to catch up to where he was later.

"Have you seen Eldon lately?" Arabella asked her handmaiden.

"No, Lady Arabella," her handmaiden answered.

"Strange," Arabella said, "He usually takes better care of things than this."

"Perhaps he is busy with everything that is happening with the demon," her handmaiden suggested.

"That is possible," Arabella said, "But it still seems strange."

Arabella left her son's bedroom with her handmaiden following her and headed down the hallway toward the library. She had been in the middle of a book, which would be suitable for Waldemar's lessons, yesterday and she had hoped to finish reading it today to make sure it was right for her purpose. Waldemar had missed lessons this week because his tutor had to attend a family funeral out in the country and if he did not get back next week, Arabella intended to restart Waldemar's lessons with some of the books she found on relevant subjects. When his tutor got back, she would stop her lessons. However, she felt her son needed to continue to learn even if his tutor was not available.

Arabella and her handmaiden stopped in their tracks and started to back up. In the middle of the hallway was the creature that had been described to Arabella as the demon currently terrorizing the castle. It was sniffing the air as if searching for something that it could not see. Arabella started trying doors on one side of the corridor while her handmaiden tried the other side. But everything was suddenly locked.

The demon suddenly caught whatever scent it was searching for. Arabella felt her heart rate increase. She had been in danger many times in her life and had her life threatened plenty, but never had she faced down such a being. Arabella feared for herself as well as her handmaiden. There were no guards around and no one to stop this thing from attacking. She had a dagger hidden in her dress, but she very much doubted it would do her any good.

Except that the demon did not fix on Arabella, but her handmaiden. Arabella wondered at that for a brief moment before grabbing her handmaiden's hand and urging her to run. The handmaiden had frozen when the demon fixed on her, but she had the sense to run when Arabella grabbed her hand. They headed in the opposite direction from the demon. However, there was a snarl and then Arabella could hear the padding of feet on the floor, which sounded kind of like a lizard. Arabella glanced over her shoulder. The demon was after them. Their choices were limited. They could try to outrun it and hoped it would lose interest in them. They could find a door that was unlocked, but Arabella had been sure all these doors had been a mere minute ago. There were no stairs to take them down to any place where they could get help, but Arabella remembered a secret Hillel had shown her shortly after they had moved into the castle.

Arabella sped up and her handmaiden kept pace. She tugged her handmaiden over to the left side of the hallway. A glance back showed that the demon was gaining on them. Arabella stopped at the place she knew. Her handmaiden tried to keep running, but Arabella pulled her to a stop. There was a stone in the wall that was a slight shade darker than the rest of them. Arabella pushed it in and part of the wall swing out, leaving enough space for the women to slip inside. The wall closed up behind them and the demon was locked out. They could hear it start scratching on the wall as they caught their breath.

"I never knew about this," the handmaiden said, "Where are we, Lady Arabella?"

"Come on," Arabella pulled on the handmaiden's hand, "There are no lights in this part." Arabella went along to the left by feel as it was too dark to see anything. Her handmaiden followed.

They came to a set of stairs going up. This confused the handmaiden even more because there was not really another floor above that one. The stairs climbed steadily and must have led to somewhere well above that floor. There was no sound of the demon getting through the wall and chasing after them. Since nothing had prevented the demon until now, the handmaiden was not sure why the wall did, or whether it was playing with them.

Arabella had not been on these stairs in a long time, but the height and distance up were so familiar she had no problem following them up and around as they spiralled up. Hillel had told her that nothing could get at her here, though how he knew about them she did not know, nor did she understand what he meant. She only hoped it meant that the demon was stuck on the other side of that wall. There were no landings to stop at and there was no light coming from anywhere. It did not matter if their eyes were open or closed though the mind played tricks in thinking that it was getting used to the dark.

The castle steward had a guard following him around as he went room to room and told people to leave their posts to gather in the throne room. Many of them assumed that Weldon was going to make some sort of announcement, but a few understood there was something dangerous in the castle and this was for their safety. The castle steward had slowly been making his way up the stairs. One of the people he had not come across all morning was Lady Arabella and her handmaiden. Likely they were spending the day in the library, thinking it was safe there.

When the castle steward was finally passed the rooms where people were likely to be, he was free to head straight up to the library. The guard continued to follow him. They reached the library and the castle steward entered first.

"Lady Arabella?" the castle steward called. He did not get an answer. He went one way and the guard went the other. They met up at the chairs in front of the window. There was no one in the library.

"She might still be in bed," the castle steward said as he headed for the door. The guard followed.

Once out of the library, the castle steward broke into a

run because Lady Arabella never slept this late. They reached the hallway where Lady Arabella's room was along with Waldemar's room. The door to Waldemar's room was open, so the castle steward looked in there first. It was empty of both the boy and his mother. The castle steward went across the hallway and knocked on Lady Arabella's door. There was no answer, so he opened it. It was empty as well.

The castle steward did a quick search but found nothing that suggested to him where they were. The guard followed him back out into the hallway. The castle steward headed down the hallway just in case there was something down there. He was going at a quick pace when his foot slipped on something and he just about fell. This stopped both of them as they studied the hallway before moving forward. There were puddles along this part of the hallway and led further down to a place where there were scratches on the wall. The marks looked like they were likely made by the demon. It had tried to get through the wall there, but could not do it. The guard looked confused by this.

"What was it trying to get to?" the guard asked.

"I am not sure," the castle steward answered, "But it does not look like it got whatever it was after."

"Maybe it was Lady Arabella and her handmaiden," the guard said.

"Then where did they go?" the castle steward asked, "As far as I know there is nothing behind that wall."

"Let us try," the guard said. He pushed in the area, where the demon had scratched, but nothing moved. He tapped on it, but it sounded solid. He felt around the cracks in the stone, but none of them seemed out of place or able to be pressed in. The castle steward looked over the rest of the wall, but he did not see any sign of anything that might make a wall move. Finally, the guard gave up.

"What now?" the guard asked the castle steward.

"We continue to look for Lady Arabella and her handmaiden," the castle steward answered, "And hope we find them before the demon does."

"Yes, sir," the guard said as they started down the rest of the hallway to search the rooms down there.

The handmaiden followed Arabella up the stairs. They could no longer hear the demon or anything else from below. It was still too dark to see where they were going, or if there was anything else in this staircase. Arabella continued to find her way based on memories from days long passed. The last time she had been in here, she had been in love with her husband and excited about their new life with him being king. She thought she knew him then and she was sure he was going to be a great king. After all, once the people got to know him as she did, he would be the favourite. Unfortunately, she did not know him like she thought she had. He had turned out to be a complete stranger to her.

"How far up are we going, Lady Arabella?" her handmaiden's voice interrupted Arabella's thoughts.

"Should not be too far now," Arabella answered.

"Can the demon get in here?" her handmaiden asked, "Because the stories from yesterday made it sound like the demon could get anywhere it wanted without regard to walls and other such."

"We are safe in here," Arabella answered, "If the demon was scratching at the wall it means he could not get in and get us."

"Most would not have saved me, but would have left me to the demon while they saved themselves," her handmaiden said, "So, thank you for saving me."

"It was the right thing to do," Arabella said, "From the looks of things, it was after you and not me."

"But why?" her handmaiden asked, "I am nothing."

"I do not know," Arabella answered, "It went after the cook's daughter yesterday. It does not seem to care whether a person is a servant or not. Without knowing what it is after, it is hard to know who is a likely target. Different demons go after different things."

"What kind of demon is it?" her handmaiden asked.

"I do not know," Arabella answered, "I really only have experience with one kind of demon and I had hoped I would never have to face another one in my lifetime."

"Would it have killed me?" her handmaiden asked.

"I do not know," Arabella answered, "The last demon just killed people outright and did not take them away. Once this one takes a person away, I do not know what it does to that person. For all I know it likes to feed in private."

Her handmaiden shivered and did not ask any more questions. Arabella remembered the door must have been coming up. She put out her hand to see if she could find it before she ran into it. There was another half turn of the staircase before her hand connected with the wooden door. She let go of her handmaiden's hand to try the handle on the door. Her handmaiden whimpered, but Arabella knew she would be all right. A twist of the handle and the door opened. Light from inside spilled out into the staircase and they were able to see. Her handmaiden sighed while Arabella opened the door the rest of the way and stepped inside. This was two small rooms, which were in a tower that was at the back of the castle and faced out toward the wall. Through the window in which the sun shone, there was a beautiful view of the forest, which stretched out forever as far as anyone looking could tell. This room was the sitting room and the other one was a bedroom. Neither of them had any dust and were always neat.

Arabella remembered coming up with Hillel a couple times and there was always clean sheets on the bed, even though Hillel claimed no servants ever came up here. He said no one knew about this place and that it was safe from detection. Since the demon could not come in, Arabella believed him. However, she felt there was something strange about it all. Like if no one know about these rooms, how did he find them?

Arabella's handmaiden stepped inside and closed the door. She was looking around in wonder.

"Where are we?" her handmaiden asked.

"The back tower," Arabella answered.

"What back tower?" her handmaiden asked.

"We should be safe here," Arabella said, "But we have no way of getting a message out to let anyone know where we are and that we are safe. We might as well get comfortable for the moment. I expect the demon will be elusive until Rana gets back, which should be sometime this afternoon. We will head down about supper time and hope the demon is off looking for something else."

"Okay, Lady Arabella," her handmaiden said as she sat down on the sofa.

Arabella sighed before sitting down in the chair across from the girl.

The castle steward and the guard searched all the rooms from that floor on down to the main level. They did not come across anyone else and they did not find Lady Arabella and her handmaiden. Weldon and the captain of the guard were standing outside the throne room when the castle steward and the guard reached it.

"Everyone cleared out of the rooms and suites?" Weldon asked.

"Yes," the castle steward answered, "Though we did not find Lady Arabella or her handmaiden. Have you seen them?"

"No, they have not arrived down here," Weldon said, "But neither had Waldemar's servant, Eldon. Are you sure they are not up there?"

"We did not see anyone up there," the castle steward answered, "But we did find traces of the demon. Puddles were leading up to a place where something was scratching at the wall. We thought maybe there was some secret hiding place behind the wall, but we could not find any way to open it and I have never heard of anything being back there."

"I do not remember any kind of secret hiding place there either," Weldon said, "Perhaps it thought it could get through the wall at that point and into the room behind."

"That is possible, I suppose," the castle steward said, "But that still leaves three people missing."

"Hopefully, they will turn up soon," Weldon said, "Everyone else is in the throne room, except the cook who claims he cannot leave the kitchen and should any demon show up there he will stuff it into the ovens and roast it. I believe he will give it a go too."

"I sent a carriage to gather Rana, but it is unlikely to get here until evening at least," the castle steward said.

"Then we will have to wait it out," Weldon said, "Hopefully if everyone is gathered together it will prevent the demon from taking any more people."

The men went into the throne room and closed the door behind them. The people inside quieted down and looked at them for an explanation. Weldon went up on the dais and turned to the crowd.

"We have a serious situation," Weldon announced, "There is a demon running loose in the castle and our attempts to find and get rid of it have not succeeded so far. We hope to have better luck and more information this evening. However, until then we need everyone to stay here, where we hope it will be safe. If you have any concerns or have noticed that anyone is missing, please let me, the castle steward, or the captain of the guard know about it. If that person is in the marketplace or in town, the guards at the gates are turning everyone away as the demon has not yet been seen in town. We know this is not the ideal solution to this situation, but please be patient as it is the best we can do in the circumstances. Thank you."

Weldon stepped down and after a moment, people began to talk among themselves before settling in some corner of the room with the blankets the castle steward had arranged to have brought in for the occasion. The three men stood by the door so people could come talk to them as needed.

Many came over to tell them about their child, or children, who were missing. Weldon noted each one on his sheet of who all was missing. A few came over to say their co-worker was missing, but many of them admitted that they did not know if the person had even arrived at the castle before the gates were closed. By the time people stopped coming, there were still the same three people confirmed as missing and about fifteen children gone.

WALDEMAR AND THE CHILDREN TRY TO GET OUT WHILE THE ADULTS TRY NOT TO PANIC OVER THE SITUATION

Waldemar regained consciousness to the sound of water dripping in the distance. He sat up ad looked around. Wherever this place was, it appeared to be the cellar of a large building. There were lanterns on the walls, which gave off enough light for him to see his surroundings without any problems. The ceiling and walls were dull grey stone while the floor was packed dirt. There were three wooden doors off this room though not much else. A table had been put in the centre of the room, but it was merely big enough to be used as a workstation and there were no chairs to sit on. The source of the water dripping was not in sight. The other children were lying on the floor around Waldemar and were starting to stir as whatever spell was lifting.

Getting to his feet, Waldemar carefully avoided stepping on anyone as he went to each door to check on them. The first one was locked and bolted. There was no way through this door, except with several keys and being on the other side. Waldemar figured that this was the door to the stairs, which went up into the main building. There was no sign as to what the building was or what the cellar was used for.

Waldemar went to the next door. It opened into a room with casts for wine. As they appeared to be mostly unopened, Waldemar figured they were either in someone's house, or a tavern was above them. He went into the room, but he could not find anything worthwhile. Waldemar closed the door on his way out. He went to the next door and opened it. Behind this one was a smaller room, which was dark and dank and appeared to be where the demon lived. There were several sets of bones from people who had already been victims of the demon.

As much as he did not want to do it, Waldemar stepped into the room and examined the bones. The cleanest one wore clothing matching that of Bethany, the cook's daughter. Waldemar remembered her helping him and some of the rest finding their way around the market for the first few visits. She had not been able to go for several months because she had gotten work somewhere in the castle, which took up a lot of her time. She had also reached the age when accompanying children to the market was not as attractive as the stable boy, who definitely had an interest in her. Waldemar was sorry she was dead.

Two more skeletons were lying on the floor. The ones slightly under what used to be Bethany wore a brown outfit with the crest of a royal servant. Waldemar took a closer look and realized that the bones belonged to Eldon. The outfit matched what Waldemar had last seen Eldon wearing. Waldemar struggled to hold in his emotions. He would never have believed Eldon was dead if the bones were not right there in front of him. Eldon was always there to clean up messes and provided what he could for support. There were certain things he could not do, but he did what he could and Waldemar felt like he would always be there. Now he was gone.

Waldemar hesitated before examining the third skeleton because he was not sure he wanted to know who it was. However, a cursory glance at the clothes showed that the person had been a servant in one of the noble houses near the castle. He had seen the colours many times but had never paid much attention to it. Waldemar was sure that they had no children his age. Otherwise, he would have remembered them much better. He wondered if the servant was from the house they were trapped in the cellar of. Since that was the last set of bones in here, perhaps the rest of the household were alive and could unlock the door to set them free.

It would be difficult to make enough noise for anyone to hear them from the cellar, but Waldemar was sure they could find some way of being heard. He turned to leave the room and found Damon standing there and looking in.

"They are dead, are they not?" Damon asked.

"Yes, they are dead," Waldemar answered.

"And we are going to share their fate," Damon said.

"I think we can escape," Waldemar said taking his friend by the shoulders and leading him out of the room. Waldemar closed the door before facing the group of children who looked terrified.

"How can we escape?" Damon asked.

"I believe we are in the cellar of one of the nobility near the castle," Waldemar answered, "And all we need to do it to attract their attention. Once they hear us, they will open the door and we can get out."

"What if they are in league with the demon?" Damon asked.

"Then we will find that out when they come tell us to keep it down," Waldemar answered, "All the nobility in the city have regular visitors and no one wants prisoners making a racket while there are guests about. But since we are in the cellar, we need to make a lot of noise to be heard."

"What should we do to make noise?" Damon asked.

"Bang on the walls with anything metal you can find," the girl who answered was slightly older than Waldemar and was the daughter of one of the guardsmen who stood out at the gate. She had been around as long as Waldemar could remember and usually had enough common sense to get out any situation. He thought her name might be Jessica.

Everyone started to search around for anything metal to use. Many had things in their pockets and some objects had gotten lost in corners, but a few were still missing something to use. Waldemar with some help from Jessica and Damon took down one of the lanterns. They took as much of the metal off as possible without spilling any of the oil or putting out the flame.

When everyone was ready and positioned beside a wall, Waldemar gave the signal and everyone started rapping their metal object against the wall as loud as possible. A few were adding their own shouts to the noise level. However, those ones grew hoarse very quickly and had to stop. They continued to pound on the wall though and the sound must have been loud enough to be heard throughout the house. It might even have been enough to wake someone if it was night time. But Waldemar could not be sure of that as he was right in the middle of the noise and not in the upper part of the house.

There was no noise from the upper part of the house. There were no footsteps, or people moving, or items being dropped, or music, or food being cooked. There were no sounds of anyone coming down the stairs. And there were definitely no sounds of the door being unlocked. If the people upstairs could hear them, they were being ignored.

After a while, the children grew tired of making the noise, but Waldemar did not want to give up on it all together. Instead, he gave five of them the heaviest of the metal objects and had them knock on the door, which lead up to the stairs. They would change if anyone got too tired, but the sound could continue.

Several others sat on the floor and rested. They did not see much else they could do given the circumstances and they were tired. Waldemar, Damon, Jessica, and anyone else who was interested stood around the table and tried to think of another way to get out of this cellar. One of the other boys had a pocket knife, but that was the only weapon among them. No one had anything to dig with, or to use to pry the door open. Some of the metal pieces might be useful to try and chip away at the door, but no one believed they could make enough progress to get through it within anything less than a week. Since there was no source of food and the water was dripping into the room the demon had picked for its own and no one really wanted to drink it.

"I have an idea," Jessica said, "We do not have to chip at the door to make a hole in it."

"Why not?" Damon asked.

"We have the flame from the lantern," Jessica answered, "We can just burn the door down and get through it that way."

"Great idea," Waldemar said, "We just place this lantern near the bottom corner and hopefully it will be close enough to cause the wood from the door to burn."

"Then let us try it," Damon said.

Waldemar picked up the lantern from the table and took it to the door. Those making noise stopped to watch him.

"We are going to stop making the noise for a short while," Waldemar told them, "We need to give the flame some space to prevent us from getting hurt."

The ones who had been making noise nodded and then went over to join the others. Damon, Jessica, and the rest also went to sit on the floor with the rest of the group. Waldemar placed the lantern's flame as close to the wooden corner of the door as he could before going to sit with the others. Everyone watched the flame, but it did not seem to do anything at first.

After several minutes, smoke started to gather in the air. Waldemar realized there was going to be a problem with the smoke.

"Cover your mouths and stay as low as possible," Jessica's voice came from where she was sitting behind him. Waldemar was grateful as he pulled his shirt up over his mouth and laid down directly on the floor. Everyone else did similar. It made it difficult to watch the flame's process, but Waldemar turned on his side so he could see it.

The bottom of the door was starting to turn black near where the flame was, but there was nothing else happening. Slowly the black spot grew, but there was something that appeared to be dripping off the door. It was dripping down on the floor beside the lantern, but a little to the right and it would be dripping into the lantern and likely to put the flame out. Waldemar hoped it would not put the flame out,

Whatever was dripping seemed to be making it harder for the door to burn, but once it had melted off the wood of the door burned easily. Both produced more smoke, which filled the air and caused Waldemar to have trouble seeing the door though the flame was visible as a bright point in all the greyness. Despite the shirt over his mouth, Waldemar could still feel the tickle of the smoke reaching his lungs and the urge to cough. The others behind him were also started to cough. Waldemar realized they needed to get out of the smoke. His thoughts went to the room with the casts of wine.

Waldemar got to his knees and crawled over to the group. He started tugging on Jessica's sleeve. She looked at him and he point in the direction of the door. Then he moved on to Damon and did the same. Damon looked a little confused, but Jessica understood. She started directing everyone in the direction Waldemar had pointed while heading there herself. Waldemar continued his route through the bodies. Some of them saw others headed off and followed them without prompting, but the rest Waldemar directed.

Damon had not followed Jessica but instead helped Waldemar get the rest headed toward the room. Finally, they thought they had all of them and Damon followed while Waldemar did another check. They had indeed found them all, so Waldemar headed toward the door. He reached it and closed it after him as he was the last one inside. Some of the smoke had followed them, but it was minor compared to what was still coming off the door as it was burning.

Jessica and Damon had most of the children sitting up against the barrels. Some of them were still coughing as they tried to clear their lungs of smoke. Waldemar felt like collapsing, but he made sure everyone else was all right and that there was no one missing before sitting down near the door.

There was only one lantern in this room, so it was much darker causing the children to stay together and as close to the light as they could. Waldemar doubted there was anything else in this room aside from the barrels of wine, but he really did not know for sure and he could not borrow the light to investigate. Jessica was trying to start a game to distract from the fire burning outside, but she was not having much success. Damon just sat there and tried to calm himself down.

"How about a story?" Waldemar asked the group. Everyone turned their attention to him. He thought about reaching into his pocket and getting out the Thomas Merritt book but decided that there were too many similarities to this situation than most people would be comfortable with.

"Great idea," Jessica said.

"But I am going to need everyone's help with this story," Waldemar said, "Because I am really not good at coming up with things to go into a story."

There were nods from all around as everyone settled in for the story.

"Once upon a time," Waldemar started, "There lived a…"

"Gremlin," a girl spoke up.

"There lived a gremlin," Waldemar said, "Who was not a nasty gremlin, but very polite, cheerful, and clean gremlin. His life's ambition was the collect…"

"Buttons," a boy said.

"His life's ambition was to collect more buttons than anyone else," Waldemar said, "But he was careful about the buttons he collected. It had to have fallen off the clothing and he could not pull it off. This gremlin's name was..."

"Dalton," a boy said.

"And Dalton lived in..." Waldemar said.

"An art gallery," a girl said.

"Dalton lived in an art gallery," Waldemar said, "One day Dalton was scurrying around the art gallery in search of more buttons when he found something that looked like a button but was not a button. It was a ..."

"A copper piece," a boy said.

"It was the right size and shape of a button, but it was too heavy," Waldemar said, "This must be what the humans refer to as a copper piece, Dalton thought. He liked the feel and the heft of it, so Dalton dragged it back to his nest."

"What is a heft?" a boy asked.

"Heft is how much it weighs in your hand," Waldemar answered, "Like when you pick up a rock and it fits perfectly in your hand."

"Oh," the boy nodded.

"Dalton dragged the copper piece back to his nest for safe keeping and to add to his collection," Waldemar said, "The problem was that Dalton favoured the copper piece over all his buttons and began to sit and rub it rather than go out and search for more buttons. He would venture out once a day to see if there were any buttons to collect, but it would be brief and only once because he did not like to leave the copper piece alone too long. And then one day..."

Everyone was quiet as they thought about what could happen to this gremlin, Dalton, and the copper piece. The smoke still hung in the air, but there seemed to be less of it now. Waldemar did not dare to open the door again to see what was happening with the fire as it would let more smoke in, which was not something he wanted.

"He found a silver piece," a girl spoke up from the back of the group.

"And then one day during his outing looking for buttons, he came across a silver piece," Waldemar said, "This was even prettier than the copper piece he already had. Dalton took it back to his nest. His button collection was fairly large, but his favourite pieces were the copper and silver ones. He took special care of them, but he continued to go out and search the art gallery for more pieces. Buttons he accepted, but he hoped for more copper and silver pieces. His button collection got bigger, but he did not find any more copper or silver pieces. Then one day Dalton came back to his nest and found…"

"The pieces were stolen," a boy near Waldemar said.

"Then one day Dalton came back to his nest and found that the copper and silver piece had been stolen from him," Waldemar said, "He searched everywhere behind the wall, where his nest was, but he could not find them anywhere. Dalton went out into the art gallery to search there when…"

"He sees the cat," a boy said.

"Dalton went out into the art gallery to search for his copper and silver piece when he saw a cat the art gallery owner had recently acquired," Waldemar said.

"What is acquire?" a girl asked.

"It means to buy something or be given it," Waldemar said.

"Oh," the girl replied.

"This cat was sitting up on a bench in the art gallery looking around for mice the art gallery owner was sure were around," Waldemar said, "Dalton made his way back to his nest as slowly as possible without taking his eyes off the cat. However, the cat spotted him before he could disappear back through the hole. Dalton watched the cat lick its lips and get ready to spring. He no longer worried about slowness or being sneaking. He just turned and ran for it. The cat went after him. Dalton reached the hole mere second before the cat got him and was able to run far enough in that the cat barely grazed his backside with its claws. He scrambled farther away and the cat tried several more times to get him. Dalton found himself a place to sit and check his wounds. He also had to think about his situation for a little while. The cat was unlikely to go away as the art gallery owner had gotten it for the purpose of getting rid of Dalton. His button collection was going to take a lot of work to move. And he really would have liked a chance to find his missing copper and silver pieces, which the cat likely stole from his nest. He was glad his button collection was far enough in that the cat could not get at it.

The cat quit pawing around the hole and withdrew, but Dalton could tell that the cat was outside waiting for him to be foolish enough to step outside. He was smart enough that he was not going to let the cat just get him. Instead, Dalton searched for his bag. He had dropped it in the back of the wall when he had arrived and unpacked. Now he needed to see how much of his button collection he could fit in it. He was also going to have to figure out where to move to, but that would have to wait until tomorrow.

Dalton found his bag and packed as many buttons into as he could before falling asleep. The next morning, he took his bag and left the art gallery. He wandered the town for a long time until he found..."

"A mill," a girl said.

"Dalton wandered the town for a long time until he

came across a mill, which had a large and empty loft," Waldemar said, "After making sure it was all right with the horse, Dalton moved in. It took several trips to get all his buttons from the art gallery, but eventually he had them all moved. The Miller and his wife were pleasant people and never noticed their new tenant, but they did lose buttons. Dalton was able to keep collecting buttons and making his collection bigger. Occasionally he found buttons on the road to the mill, even.

One day Dalton was doing his usual wander in search of buttons when he found a copper piece. This time, Dalton knew exactly what it was and there was no mistaking it for a button. Dalton did not pick it up, but with the memory of the cat still in his mind ran home and left the copper piece for the Miller to find. The Miller put it in his pocket and whistled his way home. The end."

The children applauded the story. Jessica took over and organized a game while Waldemar went to the door and listened. He was sure he could still hear the crackling of the door burning, but he could not quite be sure and he could not open the door. So Waldemar joined in with Jessica's game to keep everyone's moral up.

By the time the game was over, everyone was tired and hungry. A few still had food left from breakfast that was shared around, but it was a small amount. Waldemar himself wished he had taken a little more to eat later, but he had thought later would be lunch and that there was nothing to worry about. He supposed now that more guards wandering the courtyard should have tipped him off that something was wrong in the kingdom. Weldon was good about keeping Waldemar in the loop as to what was happening in the kingdom, but with Waldemar's tutor being away he had been so busy spending time with his friends that he was not around to hear what was happening. He regretted it this time. After all, Weldon must have known about the demon and Waldemar had not even been around to warn about it.

Once everyone had eaten something, they all laid down. Tiredness and fear were combined with a long day. Waldemar continued to sit up and watch over the rest. Damon was the first one asleep, but Jessica was still awake and sitting up. Slowly the children fell asleep leaving only Waldemar and Jessica awake.

"Thank you for your help," Waldemar said, "I think there were several times when things might have fallen into chaos if you had not stepped in."

"You are welcome," Jessica said, "Your idea of telling a story using their suggestions worked like magic."

"That is what would have worked to calm me down in such a circumstance," Waldemar said, "So, I thought it would work for some others. I first had the idea to read from the book I have with me, but I thought that might be too scary based on where we are."

"That was the book you were reading to Damon earlier?" Jessica asked.

"Yes, it is," Waldemar answered.

"I was listening to a little bit then," Jessica said, "It sounded interesting, but yes, you are right, it would not have worked well to calm the group down. But the story about the gremlin worked perfectly."

"Thank you," Waldemar said, "Adventures for a Future King likely gave me the idea."

"It must be a interesting book," Jessica said.

"You can read it when I am done," Waldemar said.

"No," Jessica shook her head.

"Why not?" Waldemar asked.

"I cannot read," Jessica answered.

"I can teach you to read," Waldemar said, "Then you

can read the book."

"I would like to learn, but I doubt I will get to use that skill in my life," Jessica said.

"It does not matter whether you will use it much," Waldemar said, "It is important to learn so you can enjoy books for themselves. I will teach you to read when we get out of this and you can borrow books from the library to read."

"I am supposed to start working in the laundry next week," Jessica said.

"We can arrange a time for you to learn once you know about the times when you are expected to be there," Waldemar said.

"Okay," Jessica said, 'But we should probably get some sleep so we are ready when the door finishes burning."

"You sleep," Waldemar said, "I will keep watch for a while. I will wake Damon to keep watch before I fall asleep. I do not want to leave us unguarded in case the demon comes back."

"Very well," Jessica said. She laid down and closed her eyes, but she did not immediately go to sleep. Waldemar reached over and took her hand in his. He squeezed it gently and she squeezed back. Then she drifted off to sleep.

Waldemar sat there in a room full of sleeping people and wondered if this was what being a king really meant. To be the guard in the room of people and protect them from things that would harm them. He seemed to be good at it, if it was. His mother never told him stories of his father's reign, nor did Weldon. His tutor told him stories from the reign of King Proster, the man who took the kingdom over and founded the kingdom of Proster. Occasionally someone would tell him a story from the reign of his grandfather, Driscoll. But his father was never mentioned to him and Waldemar wondered what kind of king he had been. Had he helped the people? Had he kept them from harm? Had he been what they needed protection against?

Waldemar felt his eyes start to close, but he fought it. He got up and did a short walk around to keep himself awake before sitting back down again. This helped for a little while, but again he found feel sleep creeping up on him. Waldemar knew he should wake Damon and get him to keep watch for a while. When Damon could not keep awake any longer, then he would wake Waldemar up again. Waldemar's eyes closed as he thought about waking Damon up. His mind continued in its thought pattern as in his dream he did wake Damon and give him the instructions before letting himself slip off to sleep.

The white wolf was pulling on Waldemar's sleeve. He wanted to fear the creature, but the blue eyes made him feel that there was nothing to be afraid of from the creature. It was trying to help him. But right now, it wanted him to follow it. Waldemar got to his feet and walked over the children to follow the white wolf, who had no trouble moving around the bodies without stepping on them. The air was clear of smoke in the larger room. When Waldemar looked the door was still intact.

The white wolf tugged to make Waldemar go towards the room the demon had claimed for its own purposes. Waldemar was not sure he wanted to go that way, but the white wolf did not give him a choice. The room was almost as he had last seen it. There was a new skeleton on the floor that had not been there before. This one wore the same outfit as Jessica had been wearing, but Waldemar remembered seeing in the room with the rest of the children less than a moment before.

Also, in the room was the demon and it was hissing at him.

The white wolf nudged Waldemar's pocket until he took out the pocket knife. Then the white wolf charged at the demon and attacked the thing's neck. However, the demon did not act like it had a white wolf attached to its neck. It was like the white wolf did not exist to the demon. The white wolf let go of the demon's neck and looked at Waldemar expectantly. Waldemar realized the white wolf was showing him what he had to do.

Waldemar took a deep breath and charged the demon. He stabbed the demon in the neck with the pocket knife. He pulled the knife out to stab again, but the demon disappeared. Waldemar looked around and found the white wolf had disappeared as well. He was not sure what to do when there was a hiss from somewhere in the distance.

The sound of something sliding across the floor caused Waldemar to jerk awake. He looked around and found everyone else asleep. Damon was in the same position he had been when he had fallen asleep. The only one missing was Jessica. At first, Waldemar thought she might be keeping watch somewhere else and then the sliding noise penetrated his still sleep clouded brain. That along with the fact that the door was open and letting smoke in, put Waldemar on alert. He scrambled to his feet and out the door while keeping low enough to avoid breathing in too much smoke.

He saw Jessica was unconscious as she was being dragged into the other room by the demon. Waldemar ran to catch up, but she had been pulled into the room before he could get there. Instead, he reached the doorway as the demon leaned over her with it mouth open and dripping saliva all over her. A tongue was extending out of the mouth and attached itself to Jessica's neck. She jerked once and then was still.

Waldemar screamed as he ran at the demon with the

pocket knife in his hand. The demon did not respond, at first, probably thinking that Waldemar was not a threat. Waldemar managed to get the pocket knife into the demon's neck and twist it around. The demon pulled back with a screech causing Waldemar to pull the pocket knife out. The demon stumbled back and Waldemar followed it looking for another chance to attack it again. Before he could connect with the demon again, it disappeared.

Waldemar made sure it was gone before rushing to Jessica's side. He checked for a pulse, but there was not one. He started trying every method he knew to restart a heart, but nothing worked. She remained lifeless. The demon did not have time to suck her dry as the bones littering the floor nearby, but it had managed to kill her. Jessica's eyes were closed and she looked like she was just asleep.

Waldemar remembered one of his first tutors talking about people not truly being dead, but merely become a hollow shell with the soul going to paradise. The soul was with friends and waiting for the rest to finish their time on this plane. He wondered now whether that was actually true. Was Jessica in paradise? Would she wait for him to finish his time on this plane so they could be friends there where no demons were trying to kill them? He hoped so, she deserved a place where she could learn to read and did not have to work in the castle laundry.

There was a gasp from the doorway. Waldemar looked up to see Damon standing there.

"It came back, did it not?" Damon asked.

"Yes," Waldemar nodded. He felt his chin was wet and wiped away the droplets only to discover they started at his eyes and ended up there. He wiped his whole face with his sleeve as he got to his feet.

"We need to figure out a way out of here before it comes back," Waldemar said, "None of the rest of us should be a meal for that thing."

Damon just nodded and Waldemar pushed passed him and into the room. He went over to the door, which was still smouldering at its hinges, but most of the rest of the door had been burned up. The smoke was still strong and thick. Waldemar went around any part of it that still looked hot and found a set of stairs going up. Damon was behind him as he went up the stairs. There were no lanterns along the stairs themselves, but there was one that could be seen at the top of the stairs.

It was a long staircase, which caused Waldemar to wonder if the residents could have heard the noise they had made yesterday. Finally the two boys reached the landing at the top. The light from the lantern showed a steel door, which looked very thick and was locked as well. Waldemar tried the handle and both boys pushed against it, but it was not moving. Waldemar took out the pocket knife and Damon took out one of the pieces of the lantern, which looked like it could have been used as a weapon, and they both started banging on the door.

It was loud and this time Waldemar was sure it could not have been ignored. They knocked for a good long time, but without any answer. Even if the nobles from this house were in league with the demon they would still have answered the door to send the boys back down to the cellar and to stop the banging, which would be interrupting their lifestyle. Some of the other children came to the staircase and looked up, but they did not climb the stairs as it was obvious as to what the banging was.

After a while of banging, Waldemar and Damon stopped.

"What do we do now?" Damon asked.

"I do not know yet," Waldemar answered, "But we need to go down and calm the rest. Maybe someone else has an idea that we could use."

"Okay," Damon said. He got up and headed back down the stairs while Waldemar stayed seated. Damon did not look back to see if his friend was coming but just continued going down.

Though Arabella had offered the bed to her handmaiden, the girl refused it saying she would be far more comfortable on the sofa with the spare blanket. Arabella had laid there most of the night staring out at the stars wondering where her son was and whether he was safe. She had never gotten as far as the dining room or talking to the castle steward, or even Weldon. She did not know if the children had been allowed to go back to the marketplace, or whether someone felt it was better if they stayed within the gates. She had hoped that they had been allowed to go to the marketplace. Arabella was not sure why, but she felt that Waldemar was safer in the marketplace than the castle, though she did not understand why she felt that way.

Now that the sun was up, Arabella found she had at some point fallen asleep and her head was now fuzzy with sleep. She knew she was safe, but she wanted to find Waldemar and know for sure that he was safe. If he had gone to the market place yesterday, he would have come back last evening and might even have been looking for her. She also needed to talk to the castle steward and Weldon.

She got and splashed her face with the water, which was in the wash basin near the window. She wiped her face off before going into the sitting room. Arabella knew she looked like she had slept in her clothes, but there were more important things to get done. Her handmaiden was still sleeping on the sofa. Arabella leaned down and shook the girl's shoulder. The handmaiden sat up and blinked as she looked around.

"It is morning," Arabella said.

"Of course, I am so sorry for sleeping in, Lady Arabella," the handmaiden said.

"It is fine," Arabella said, "We need to get something to eat and gather news of anything that has happened since we have been stuck up here."

"Do you think it is gone?" the handmaiden asked.

"Likely," Arabella said, "It probably went after easier prey."

The handmaiden looked nervous but got to her feet. She followed Arabella out the door and down the dark stairs. It felt like it was shorter this time, but at the same time the exit did not come soon enough as far as the handmaiden seemed concerned. Arabella remembered the distance.

When they reached the door, Arabella pushed and the wall slid open. They stepped out and Arabella pushed it closed again. It disappeared and the handmaiden did not think she could have found it again if she tried. They reached Waldemar's room and Arabella checked inside. Everything was exactly as it had been the day before. The bed did not even look like it had been slept in again.

Arabella was ready to head downstairs and start asking questions, but her handmaiden stopped her and would not let her go until she was presentable.

Weldon and the castle steward sat near the doors to the throne room as people around them were in various stages of consciousness. The captain of the guard had left a while ago to reorganize the guards. Neither Weldon or the castle steward had slept. They were both waiting for the announcement that the carriage had brought Lady Rana back, but despite expectations to the otherwise, the carriage had not arrived that evening. Now it was the next morning and still there was no word on where it was or when it was expected.

The cook had brought in some breakfast, but as most of the people were still sleeping, he did not bring much and said he would bring more later. When Weldon had asked, the Cook said everything had been quiet in the kitchen and the demon had not appeared at all. It was the same thing any guard, Weldon stopped to question had said. Was the demon gone? Or did they just stop it by gathering everyone together? Or was if after Waldemar after all?

Weldon got to his feet to stretch and have a moment to himself. The castle steward was in a semi-conscious state and did not even notice Weldon had moved. Weldon stepped out of the throne room and enjoyed the quiet and space of the corridor. His head cleared a little bit and the horror started creeping back in. The king was missing, presumed dead, his mother was missing as well, and the demon was still wandering the castle looking for victims. Daniella was probably worried about him and questioned why he had not come home, especially since it was not far to their house. Or maybe she had noticed the guards turning people away from the gates. He wanted to go home and wrap his arms around her. Maybe if he held her tight enough, this would all turn into a dream and everything would be all right.

Footsteps coming toward him made Weldon look up. A piece lifted off his heart at the sight of Lady Arabella and her handmaiden coming toward him.

"Weldon," Lady Arabella said, "What happened? Where is Waldemar? It does not look like his bed was slept in." Weldon felt his heart sink again as he knew he could not lie to her.

"The children were not let out to go to the market place yesterday," Weldon said, "So, they went to the alcove outside the kitchen to play. Next thing anyone knew the whole group of them were gone and they had not been seen leaving the alcove."

"The demon has my son!" Lady Arabella looked like she wanted to reach out and grip his shirt collar to shake him until Waldemar appeared, but her calm demeanour reappeared.

"We gathered everyone else in the throne room to prevent anyone else from going missing," Weldon said, "But it has not been seen and we could find no trace of you."

"The demon came after us yesterday morning when we were headed down for breakfast," Arabella said, "We had to hide in a place Hillel had showed me a long time ago, which the demon could not get into. I am sorry to worry you, but we were safe."

"Thank God for that blessing," Weldon said.

"I did not think you were that much of a believer," Lady Arabella said.

"I beginning to question my beliefs," Weldon replied.

"How is Daniella?" Lady Arabella asked.

"As far as I know, she is safe in our house," Weldon said, "She has been feeling under the weather lately and she decided it was better if she stayed at home for a few days."

"Good," Lady Arabella said, "Had Lady Rana arrived yet?"

"The castle steward sent a carriage to get her because

hers had broken down," Weldon answered, "We were expecting her last night, but so far there has not been any word."

"Hopefully, we hear something soon," Lady Arabella said, "In the meantime, my handmaiden and I should find some breakfast."

"The cook has cooked breakfast and delivered some earlier," Weldon said, "There is a tray just inside the throne room, you can take from."

"Thank you, Duke Weldon," Lady Arabella said before leading her handmaiden into the throne room. Weldon watched them go inside and the door close behind them. He wanted to assure her that they were doing what they could about the demon and finding her son, but empty reassurances were not what she deserved. She deserved action.

Weldon took another deep breath and let it out slowly. At least, Lady Arabella and her handmaiden were unharmed and had been safe. If only Waldemar could be found the same way, this situation would turn out well. If everyone turned out okay, that would be even better, but something inside Weldon told him that was an unrealistic dream.

The door into the castle opened and the captain of the guards stepped inside. But instead of coming toward Weldon, he opened the door the rest of the way and held it open. Half a moment had passed before Lady Rana stepped into the hallway. She glanced around briefly before heading straight to where Weldon was standing. She did not have a hair out of place and definitely did not look like she had been traveling through the night. Weldon noted that her daughter was not with her, which he found as a surprise since Lady Rana had spoken about bringing her back when she came this time. Something about time at the castle surrounded by others would do the girl some good.

"What is going on?" Lady Rana said as she swept to a stop.

"We have a demon on loose in the castle, but we cannot find its hiding place," Weldon said, "And as of yesterday, it had taken out king."

"No wonder you sent another carriage for me," Lady Rana said, "Do you know what kind of demon it is?"

"No," Weldon answered, "I have no idea how to figure that out."

"There is a book in the study," Lady Rana said, "Get everyone involved to meet me there in a few minutes. Eustace is still in the carriage along with the looking crystal Luce gave me."

"I will meet you there," Weldon said.

"May not be the best circumstance, but it is good to be home," Lady Rana said before she kissed Weldon on his cheek before heading back out to the carriage to make sure her bags went where they were supposed to.

The captain of the guard came over to Weldon.

"Conference in the study behind the throne room," Weldon told him.

"Yes, sir," the captain of the guard said before going off.

Weldon opened the door to the throne room and stepped inside. The castle steward and Lady Arabella looked up at him.

"The study in a few minutes," Weldon said. The castle steward got to his feet, but Lady Arabella moved slower. Rather than just go across the throne room, Weldon and the castle steward left by the doors and went around. Most of the population did not know about the second door to the study and those who did felt that it was okay if people did not know.

THEY FIND OUT WHAT KIND OF DEMON IT IS AND DEFEAT IT USING SOMETHING WELDON FOUND EARLIER

The door to the study had been locked when Hillel had died and since Waldemar was too young to use it. Weldon had the key and he opened the door before the castle steward followed him inside. The study needed a good dusting, but otherwise in good condition. The castle steward tried not to sneeze when Weldon moved some papers and the dust rose in a cloud.

"I should send someone into dust regularly," the castle steward said.

"I would prefer that you did not," Weldon said, "There are things in here that are best left undisturbed."

"Very well," the castle steward said. Lady Arabella entered the study. She looked around for a moment before dusting off a chair to take a seat.

"What happened?" Lady Arabella asked.

"Lady Rana has arrived," Weldon answered, "She has Eustace with her as well as a method of contacting Luce."

"Why in here?" Arabella asked. She looked around in disgust, but it was not just the dust as she likely had memories she would rather not think about that had to do with this room.

"According to Lady Rana, there is a book on demons in here," Weldon said.

"Hillel talked about a book belonging to his father that his grandfather or great grandfather wrote," Lady Arabella said.

"And you did not mention this before, Lady Arabella?" the castle steward asked.

"He said it went missing," Lady Arabella answered, "He could not find it when he wanted it."

"That does not mean it is missing," Lady Rana said gliding into the study with the captain of the guard following her and Eustace perched on her shoulder, "Luce has suggested that the book has some intelligence, which made it hide in Hillel's presence."

"That makes it much more intelligent than some of us," Lady Arabella said.

"Good things came from Hillel existence," Lady Rana said, "You are here and your son is being raised to be a proper king.'

"If we can find him and get him back," Weldon said, "Where is this book?"

"Should just be on the shelf," Lady Rana said as she went over. She looked over the shelf and then pulled out a green leather bound book. There was no title on the book. She placed it on the desk before placing the crystal near it.

"Let us start with seeing if we can identify the demon," Lady Rana said as she opened the book. She slowly turned the pages of the book as Weldon, the castle steward, and the captain of the guard studied the pages.

None of the creatures looked familiar to any of them for many pages. Then Weldon saw the demon that had been giving Hillel bad advice, but it was not the one they were currently looking for.

They were getting closer to the end of the book when Weldon saw the demon.

"That one," the captain of the guard stopped Lady Rana at the correct page.

"Let us see what it is," Lady Rana said holding the book open, "It is something called a Raguna demon which is classified as a sucker because it sucks the energy out of its victims until there are only bones left. It only sucks the life out of victims who are pure and inexperienced."

"So, it likes children as victims," Weldon said, "Which makes sense that it would take all the children as all of them in a group probably looked like a feast."

"It likes to collect energy sources in its hiding place so it knows it had food when it needs it," Lady Rana said, "It counts as semi-intelligent in that it can take orders, but is most likely to wander around doing its own thing. Only walls built against demons can hold the demon out and only specific charms can stop it from disappearing and reappearing someplace else. It lives as long as it can keep its energy up. When wounded it will use energy to heal its self, except if hit in the neck which is its weak spot."

"So, how do we defeat it?" the captain of the guard asked.

"It sounds like you either cut off its head or hack at it until it runs out of energy," Lady Rana answered.

"Where is it likely to take its food?" Lady Arabella asked, "And how long between feedings? And why did it end up here?"

"It says here that the demon likes dark, cool places

with a source of water, but not too damp," Lady Rana said, "It does not say exactly how fast it needs to replenish its energy, but it most likely eats about twice a day."

"So, Waldemar could be dead, or could be the next in line to be feed on," Lady Arabella asked.

"As far as I can tell, that is about right," Lady Rana said.

"Where do we get a charm to trap it?" the captain of the guard asked.

"I do not know," Lady Rana answered, "But perhaps Luce could tell us that." Lady Rana took the crystal and placed it in the palm of her hand. She waited for it to warm up while those around her shuffled their feet and tried not to be too impatient. When the crystal was finally warm enough, Lady Rana placed it back on it base and waited again. This time, the wait was much shorter. A blurry picture of Luce's face appeared in the ball.

"Yes?" Luce asked.

"There is a Raguna demon terrorizing the castle and has kidnapped King Waldemar," Lady Rana answered, "We need to find a charm that will trap it so it can be defeated."

"The charm you are looking for is an amulet," Luce answered, "It is round, gold and has a ruby in the centre. If you can get it around some part of the demon, it will not be able to escape."

"Is there anywhere in specific it would take its food?" Lady Rana asked.

"We checked the castle's dungeons and tower," Weldon said.

"That one is a much harder question to answer," Luce said, "Because of its preferences could leave it so many places it could stay. Any cellar is good enough as long as it is not too damp. But it could also make itself comfortable in any windowless rooms. Also, the stalking ground of a Raguna demon is relatively large so it may want to give some distance between its hunting grounds and its hiding place. I would advise you to use Eustace for the actual search."

"I think that is all our questions for the moment," Lady Rana said.

"Good luck," Luce said and then he disappeared from the crystal.

"What we need to do now is track it down and trap it," the captain of the guard said, "If only we had the charm that would trap it."

Weldon's thoughts turned to the charm he found in the dungeon and how it looked like the charm Luce had described. The castle steward must have thought about it as well because he looked up at Weldon, who was already going through his pockets. He had kept trying to leave it in his room, but he always seemed to pick it up on the way out. Finally, he found it and pulled it out.

"I think this is what we need," Weldon said holding it up and resisting the urge to put it back away in his pocket.

"Where did you find that?" Lady Rana asked.

"It was in the dungeon when the castle steward and I were searching them," Weldon explained.

"Well, you have the charm," Lady Rana said, "I would suggest finding someone willing to be bait for the trap because I do not believe any of us count as pure and inexperienced."

"It went after my handmaiden yesterday morning," Lady Arabella said, "We can ask her."

"Then let us get this ready," the captain of the guard said as he started for the door. Weldon put the charm back in his pocket and followed. The castle steward trailed behind. Lady Rana put the book away before tucking the crystal into her pocket.

"Let us go find somewhere to wait this out," Lady Rana said held out her hand to Lady Arabella.

"Thank you," Lady Arabella said as she let herself be helped up. They left the study together and closed the door behind them.

Waldemar finally made it down the stairs to find the group had gathered in the room with the wine casts because there was less smoke in there. Damon had them organized somewhat, but it was mostly because they were scared of the demon and becoming its food rather than Damon's organizational skills.

"What have we come up with?" Waldemar asked as he sat down in the circle.

"We had come up with two methods that might work," Damon answered, "The first is to see if we can get through the lock with the pocket knife. The other is to see if we can chip away at the mortar between the stones near the door enough that we can pull the stone out."

Waldemar thought about those suggestions but figured neither of them would work. However, he looked around the room and realized to shoot them down would have stomped out any last morale left in the group. They were all sure they would be eaten by the demon and it was only a matter of time.

"Let us go try them," Waldemar said as he got to his feet. Damon and one other went with him, but the rest stayed behind where they could keep out of the lingering smoke.

At the top of the stairs, Waldemar handed the pocket knife to Damon because he was not sure how this process was supposed to work. Damon put the blade of the pocket knife into the hole in the handle and wiggled it around for several minutes. He kept trying, but he was not getting the lock to do anything. Finally, Damon gave up and handed the pocket knife back to Waldemar, who gave it a try. He wiggled it in the hole for a few minutes before inspecting the handle.

"This is not going to work," Waldemar said.

"Why not?" the other boy asked.

"Because we are not getting the pocket knife into the actual lock," Waldemar answered, "This door only locks or unlocks from the other side. Even if we had the key we could not use it to get out."

"Then on to the next idea then," Damon said as he took out the metal pieces from the lantern. They were much better than the pocket knife for the job because those were the sharpest, longest, and hardest objects down in the cellar. He had brought three pieces and the boy took one with Waldemar taking the other. Each boy picked a stone and chisel out.

They banged against the wall and tried to get the mortar to come out from in between the stones. Waldemar scratched the wall slightly, but none of the mortar chipped off. He looked over to see the other two having the same difficulty. Waldemar did not want to disappoint them, but the mortar was too solid to chip under the force of their blows.

"I do not think this is working," Damon said, "We need to think of something else because we are not going to escape this way."

"Let us go down and rejoin the rest of them," Waldemar said, "And see what we can think up."

The other two nodded before turning and heading back down the stairs. Everyone was waiting expectantly and to see the downcast faces of Waldemar, Damon, and the other boy brought a sense of doom.

"We could not get either technique to work," Damon announced as he sat down, "Are there any other suggestions?"

Silence met his question. No one had any more ideas on how to get out of the cellar. And now they were worried about being eaten by the demon.

"Earlier I managed to stab the demon," Waldemar said, "It bled from its neck before disappearing. If it bleeds, we can kill it."

"What?" Damon asked.

"When it comes back here we ambush it and take it down," Waldemar answered, "The metal piece of the lantern can be used as weapons and the pocket knife will be used. Maybe we could even take down another lantern. We will take it apart like the other, it will give us more weapons and maybe the lantern itself can be thrown at the demon. It might burn the thing."

"Then what?" Damon asked.

"We make noise until someone finds us," Waldemar said, "Duchess Rana is supposed to be back today and they will use her pet dragon to search for us. The dragon can find anyone no matter where they are hidden."

"That sounds like the best plan," Damon said, "Let us go get a lantern to use."

Waldemar and Damon got the lantern. Waldemar took it apart like he had the last one. All the pieces were handed out to be used as weapons, while what was left of the lantern was placed to that it could be thrown at the demon.

"Now what?" Damon asked once everyone was prepared.

"We wait," Waldemar answered, "We cannot do anything until the demon reappears."

"Could you tell another story while we wait?" one of the boys asked. Waldemar felt a cold spear go through his chest at the thought of making up another story.

"I am not sure I could think one up," Waldemar said, "But I could read some of the book I have with me."

"That will do," the boy said as everyone got comfortable. Waldemar took out Adventure for a Future King and opened it to his place. He started to read from where he had left off when they had been abducted.

Lady Arabella's handmaiden was not sure about being bait in a trap for the demon, but the captain of the guard and castle steward assured her that the demon would not actually be allowed to hurt her. So, they set her up in the hallway that she and Lady Arabella had been chased through before. Behind each door was positioned a couple guards. Weldon and the captain of the guard were waiting at the end of the hallway, just out of sight. The handmaiden sat there and tried to control her nervousness as the guards stayed alert while trying to be quiet.

The demon must have needed the energy because it was less than ten minutes from the time the trap was set to the time the demon appeared. It started towards the handmaiden with a hiss. Weldon barely had time to notice that it already had black blood coming from a wound in its neck before he jumped out and wrapped the charm around the demon's arm. The charm seemed to burn its skin and the demon backed away from Weldon while trying to dislodge the charm. It could not get rid of the charm as if back into the wall.

"Attack," the captain of the guard shouted as he followed Weldon out of hiding. Weldon got out of the way as the guards rushed in. He went to the handmaiden and got her away from the demon.

The captain of the guard and the guards hacked at the demon with their swords, but none were able to get a good shot at its neck. The demon lashed out with its claws. It got two of the guards, who were cut. They took a moment before getting up and charging again. The demon slashed at them again. This time, one of the guards was hit in the face with one of the claws and fell backward away from it.

The demon slashed out again at his attackers and caught another with his claws. The guard cried out in pain as he fell back. The guards fought harder with the captain of the guard trying for the demon's neck. Between the guards and the demon's claws, it was all but impossible to reach the demon's neck with his sword.

The demon swung his claws around him and all the guards who saw them in time moved back. A couple guards were knocked back and one had three claws leave marks. The demon screeched in frustration as it tried to disappear again. It scratched at the charm, but it could not remove it. One of the guards got back up from being knocked down and charged the demon. The demon opened its lower half of its face and before the guard could cut the demon with his sword, a tongue came out of the demon's mouth and attached itself to a bare area of skin. The guard collapsed to the floor, but the demon kept feeding.

The captain of the guard slashed at the tongue, which withdrew before it could be cut. However, the demon had sucked enough life that the guard looked like a starved corpse and the demon's injuries were healing. In a panic, the captain of the guard took a swing at the demon's neck with his sword. Put the demon scuttled back out of the way before jumping toward the captain of the guard with its claws out. The captain of the guard rolled out of the way before slashing at the demon's arms. He did not manage to cut through them but merely made some more marks on its arms. The marks healed quickly.

The captain of the guard backed off and studied the situation. His men were getting nowhere now that the demon had fed and everyone was hesitant to rush it again because of what happened. The captain of the guard remembered that the guard had been a young man, but he had not thought him that young. In his mind, the captain of the guard went over all those currently fighting the demon. None of them were as young as the one who now lay dead and hopefully none were as inexperienced.

"Men, at ready," the captain of the guard shouted. Despite the fear, the men did as ordered. The captain of the guard took the front position and held his sword out.

"Steady," the captain of the guard called. The guards raised their swords.

"Charge," the captain of the guard screamed as he started the charge. The guards followed behind him and when they were within range, they started swinging their swords at the demon. The demon tried to hold up its claws to block the sword swings, but they merely got sliced up. The captain of the guard managed to get his sword between the demon's arms and into its neck, but he got swept to one side before he could do much more. He also lost his grip on his sword, so it remained stuck there. The demon tried to dislodge it and keep anyone else from touching it. However, it did not slow the demon down.

The captain of the guard was slightly stunned as he leaned against the wall he had been pushed into by the demon. His eyes fell on the demon's neck and saw another smaller wound on the side of the demon's neck.

It was dripping with black blood when everything else was healing. The captain of the guard knew none of his men had managed to get that close to the neck. Someone must have gotten close enough to wound it. It was possible that it could have been King Waldemar in an attempt to stop himself from being supper. That thought raised the captain of the guard's spirits. If King Waldemar could injure the demon, the captain of the guard could finish it off.

The guards were continuing to cut the demon with their swords and healing those wounds was draining the demon of its energy. However, none were able to get at his sword or the demon's neck. The captain of the guard moved away from the wall and back into the fray. He grabbed the hilt of his sword and tried to get it through the demon's neck. The demon moved to avoid a sword and the captain of the guard's sword went through half the neck, which left the demon's head attached to the other half. If it had been human, it would have died, but the demon was acting like nothing had happened at all. It was, however, slowly down some more as it was losing energy. It did not seem to consider any of its attackers to be food.

One of the other guards had noticed that the captain of the guard was aiming for the neck, so the next swing he also went for the neck. The demon tried to avoid the captain of the guard's sword swing only to end up moving into the guard's swing. The sword went into the demon's neck and ripped all the through to the other side in one smooth stroke. The head rolled a small distance away and the body collapsed where it was.

Everyone was stood back and stared at the pieces.

"Good job," the captain of the guard clapped the guard on the shoulder.

"But it does not bring back the children," the guard replied.

"We will find them," the captain of the guard said, "But first we need to deal with this corpse. Take them out to the courtyard and burn them." The captain of the guard reached down and untangled the charm from the demon's arm. He put it into his pocket to give it back to Weldon later.

The guards put away their swords and started hauling the demon out of the castle. Several servants started a bonfire in the courtyard as soon as word reached them that the demon was dead, so by the time to guards got the body down there they could just throw it straight onto the flames.

Weldon stood at the entrance to the throne room and watched the demon being taken away to be burned. He was relieved, but the question was in his mind as to why it even showed up in this kingdom to start with. Did someone send it here? Were they in danger from someone who knew about demons? This one was looking specifically fed on children or similar. Did that make it a directed attack?

Lady Arabella and Lady Rana came to stand beside Weldon. He glanced at them, but both were focused on the activity in the courtyard. No one said anything as the smell of rotten meat filled the air. It was gag worthy and turned his stomach, even though his stomach had been complaining of hunger not that long ago.

"Well, that part is over," Lady Rana said.

"We need to find the children," Lady Arabella said, "They are likely to be starving and scared."

"They disappeared outside the kitchen door?" Lady Rana asked.

"Yes," Weldon answered. Before Lady Rana could move toward the kitchen, the captain of the guards came in sight. He was battered and looked tired, but he stopped where they were standing.

"The demon had a wound in its neck before we started attacking it," the captain of the guard reported.

"Could have been Waldemar," Lady Arabella said, "But did fighting back help him or cause him to be the demon's last meal?"

"If the demon fed on him, it was not the demon's last meal," the captain of the guard said, "I get to bury one of my own today."

"Our condolences," Weldon said.

"Let us go find those children," the captain of the guard said, "So that I can go talk to the man's family."

Lady Rana nodded as she started toward the kitchen with everyone else following.

They found the cook and his assistant sitting by the fire. The assistant was making sure what food was cooked stayed warm, but the cook had a bottle in his hand and a couple at his feet. Weldon saw that it was the cheap stuff and left the man alone. The cook had held up well up until now, there was no reason to disturb his grieving process.

The group went through the kitchen door into the courtyard. Weldon directed them to the alcove. Lady Rana looked around at it as the rest shuffled in. She had obviously never been here. Once everyone was in, Lady Rana took Eustace out of her pocket.

"We need you to find the children," Lady Rana told Eustace, "And this was the last place they were seen. Waldemar was among them." Eustace nodded before sniffing the air. He sneezed a couple times but went right back to sniffing around. Lady Rana had let him investigate the various areas of the alcove.

Finally, Eustace caught the scent he was looking for because off he went. His little wings fluttered as they held him up and let him fly at speed out of the alcove. Lady Rana was the first one after the small dragon with the rest not far behind. The dragon zipped across the courtyard to the gate on the left side. The guard let them out. The captain of the guard gave the guard some instructions before following the group. The guard acknowledged them before closing the gate.

Eustace headed down the street. Weldon wondered if the demon had made his space in one of the houses along here. His mind went to Daniella and he worried about her safety. But their house was on the other side of the courtyard. Eustace reached the last house on the street and scratched at the door. Lady Rana stopped at the door and let Eustace settle in her hand. She tucked him into a pocket before knocking on the door.

Everyone else stood there and waited for someone to answer. Weldon tried to remember who lived here. He thought it might be Lord Travers and his wife, but Weldon was not entirely sure. Both Lord Travers and his wife had been missing from court for some time. Rumour was that Lord Travers had a disagreement with Lord Laban and now neither of them were willing to come back to court. Since both Lord Travers and Lord Laban were never loud in their opinions on subjects and did not bother with alliances with others in court, no one had missed them enough to ask Weldon to look into their disagreement. Their absence was no more noticed than their presence.

No one answered the third time Lady Rana knocked on the door, so the captain of the guard tried the handle. The door opened easily and he pushed it open. The light coming in the door was the only light in the house. The curtains were closed and no lanterns were lit. Weldon lit the lantern beside the door and took the lead into the house.

They came across another lantern at the end of the hallway, which Weldon also lit before passing it to the captain of the guard. The hallway split at this point with one room on each side. Weldon and Lady Rana went into one room while the captain of the guard and Lady Arabella went into the other room.

The room Weldon and Lady Rana entered was the sitting room. There were three chairs on one side and two more on the other with a table sitting between them. On the table were two cups, a teapot, along with a half-empty plate of desserts. Sitting in what chair was the rotting remains of Lord Travers. In the chair across from him was what was left of Lady Travers, in roughly the same condition. Weldon could hear Lady Rana swallow. There was a large blood smear leaving the sitting room and going out a door on the other side of the room.

Weldon went alone as he walked across the room to the door. He did not really want to open it, but he did not have any choice. Carefully, Weldon opened the door and used the lantern to look inside. The current occupants of the small hallway, which led to the kitchen was what was left of the servants, or at least, that was what it looked like. Weldon did not think his stomach would handle getting close enough to tell how many people there were.

Closing the door, Weldon went back to where Lady Rana was standing. She was looked green around the gills.

"It is worse in there, is it not?" Lady Rana asked.

"It is," Weldon answered.

"Do they have any children?" Lady Rana asked.

"I do not remember off the top of my head," Weldon

answered, "I will have to look it up when we get back."

"They may want to burn down the house and start fresh," Lady Rana said.

"That will be their decision," Weldon replied.

The captain of the guard shouted for them to come quickly. Weldon and Lady Rana glanced at each other before rushing off to see what the other two had found.

They found the captain of the guard and Lady Arabella standing in front of a steel door in the servants' quarters off the kitchen, which showed no sign of what was through the other door. The captain of the guard was looking around for the key to the door.

"What is it?" Lady Rana asked.

"Listen," Lady Arabella answered. They were quiet for a moment. At first Weldon did not hear anything, then he could hear a tapping coming from behind the steel door. The door must have gone down to the cellar, which would be where the demon had made its home.

"Where is the key?" Weldon asked.

"I cannot find it," the captain of the guard answered, "But I have not found any servants either."

"This way," Weldon said leading the captain of the guard through the kitchen to the door on the other side. As soon as they stepped into the small hallway, the captain of the guard's face turned greyish and he looked like he was holding in the contents of his stomach. Weldon tried to get close enough to look for a key, but he could not do it. The captain of the guard could not get any closer without adverse effects.

"We will have to figure something else out," Weldon said. The captain of the guard nodded and then both went back to the kitchen. Both Lady Arabella and Lady Rana were focused on the door, so the captain of the guard had a moment to compose himself before they joined the ladies.

"The key is not accessible," Weldon said.

"Okay, then we will get Eustace to help," Lady Rana said as she took Eustace out of his pocket, where he apparently been eating berries of some kind since they were smeared across his face. He fluttered his wings and went to the keyhole. After taking a deep breath, Eustace breathed frost into the lock. He took another breath and, this time, there was frost visible on the lock. The captain of the guard took a hammer he had found nearby and smashed it into the lock. The lock was cold enough to shatter and the door opened without issue.

The two boys at the top of the stairs looked ready to fight until they saw who was there. They must have called down because the rest of the group of children came up the stairs. At the sight of his mother, Waldemar ran into her arms. Weldon wanted to sigh with relief over he being safely back, but there was a look in his eyes that had not been there before. It was like a hardness had formed and it was not going to go away.

The rest of the guards that the captain of the guard sent for arrived and the children were quickly escorted back to the castle. Lady Rana went with Lady Arabella and Waldemar, leaving Weldon standing at the top of the stairs. He went down along with the captain of the guard and a handful of guards. The main cellar was smoky and the wooden door was burned off. It looked like a lantern at the base of the door was the cause. It did not look like an accident, so mostly likely the children had started it in an effort to escape.

The other room off the main room had wine casts in it. There were tracks in the dirt floor that showed the children had been in here, but there was no visible damage. The children had apparently stayed out of the wine. The other door off the main room was closed. The captain of the guard opened the door itself and Weldon stood there to see what was inside. This room was where the demon had made its home. There were the remains of four bodies. The top one was a girl named Jessica, who was supposed start in the laundry next week. She looked practically untouched. Under her was the clothes the cook's daughter wore when she had been taken. Weldon could not see who was at the bottom, but the person under the cook's daughter appeared to be wearing the clothes of Waldemar's servant, Eldon.

Weldon turned away from the room as he did not think he could see any more bodies today. There would already be plenty of work for them tomorrow. He was not going to able to talk to the cook until then anyway. Weldon went up the stairs and sat down on a chair in the kitchen. Guards were going through the house for any this else that needed attention.

The captain of the guard came up at some point, but Weldon was trying to mentally deal with the horror and did not notice anyone else. Several guards also moved around, but no one was touching the bodies. Weldon could see the people who had died and flashing back to the bodies. He should have gone back to the castle to check whether Lord and Lady Travers had any children. He should be finding the families of the dead and letting them know what happened. But he just sat there and stared into space.

"Weldon," the captain of the guard called causing Weldon to look up.

"Yes?" Weldon asked.

"There is something upstairs I think you will want to see," the captain of the guard said.

"Is it another body?" Weldon was cautious as he got

to his feet.

"No," the captain of the guard answered, "But I think you should see it anyway."

"Okay," Weldon said feeling a little better about whatever he was going to see. He was not sure he could handle another body. Weldon followed the captain of the guard up the stairs. Most of the rooms had been searched by the guards and the doors were open to show regular rooms where people at one time slept. The captain of the guard went straight down to the last bedroom in the hallway. Weldon followed him a step inside the door and there they stopped to look over the room.

The room was probably used as servant quarters initially, but now it did not look anything like a bedroom. The walls were bare, except where various symbols had been painted on them. The floor was also in similar condition with a large circle in the middle of the room. The ceiling had splashes of something red on it, but it was impossible to tell whether it was paint or blood. There were some pots with paint in them. The only other thing in the room was a candle sitting in the centre of the circle.

Weldon felt a chill as he stood there and it was not completely due to his reaction to the room. This room was colder than the rest. The captain of the guards appeared to have a similar reaction as Weldon.

"Have you found anything else in here?" Weldon asked.

"Everything else is normal," the captain of the guard replied.

"Then do what you can to protect the buildings around this one," Weldon said, "And then burn it to the ground."

"Are you sure?" the captain of the guard asked.

"I do not understand or know what has been happening in here, but I do not think it was good," Weldon said, "The only way to purge the house of this stuff it to burn it. So, do not take anything, except the bodies in the cellar for proper burial, and do not let the flames stop until there is nothing left. The story will be that the residents died in the fire. No one needs to know anything else."

"Very well, Duke Weldon," the captain of the guard said, "I will have my men cleared out as soon as possible. The bodies from the cellar should be already making their way to where the guard who died is waiting for burial. Once the place had been evacuated, we will have it burning."

"Thank you," Weldon said. Both men left the room. The captain of the guard started issuing orders to his men about the bodies, the building, and the fire while Weldon left the house entirely. He headed back to the castle, where he found himself a comfortable position on the balcony.

Waldemar and the rest of the children were greeted with joy when they entered the throne room, where everyone was still waiting. The castle steward announced that supper was being served in the dining room shortly after. Both children and adults were starving and more than willing to follow the directions to go and eat.

Waldemar figured that the bodies were going to be moved and if everyone was in the dining room no one would see them, but he did not say anything because he felt it was a good idea. Supper was served, but it was not as good of quality as usual. No one commented as all the adults knew that the cook's daughter had been taken and was not among the children brought back alive.

Waldemar found his mother to be unwilling to let him out of her sight, but she was not demanding he stay right beside her. He appreciated it as he was not sure he was ready to talk to her about what happened down in the cellar. One day soon he would tell her about it, but not yet.

As soon as supper was finished, Waldemar headed up to his room with his mother trailing behind him. They reached his room and he sat down on the chair Eldon would sit on when he needed to stay in the room.

"I am not sure what happened to-" Arabella started to say as she looked around the room.

"He is not coming back," Waldemar interrupted her. She looked at him with concern but did not move towards him. She also did not try to say anything more. Waldemar sat there for several minutes remembering Eldon as he had last seen him. Eldon had been his personal servant for as long as Waldemar could remember. He may have been in that position all of Waldemar's life, but Waldemar doubted it. Those kinds of servants did not get assigned until a child is old enough to be moved out of the nursery.

Finally, Waldemar got up. He placed the adventures for a Future King back on his mother's rocking chair before stripping off his clothes and dumping them into the dirty laundry pile, while trying not to remember where that pile would go. Then he got himself into a nightshirt before climbing into bed. His mother moved the book before sitting down in the rocking chair. However, she did not open the book and start reading. Instead, she left it on the table and took one of the books from his shelve, which was full of books with fairy tales in them. Waldemar had stopped reading them because he felt he had grown out of them, but tonight he wanted to hear them because they were a familiar comfort. His mother read several of his favourites while he drifted along with the story.

When she decided that had been enough, she put the book back on the shelf and went over to Waldemar's bed. She leaned down to kiss his forehead because it looked like he had fallen asleep. She was surprised when he wrapped his arms around her neck and gave her a long hug. Arabella hugged him back.

"I love you," he whispered.

"I love you, too," she replied.

Then Waldemar let go. She kissed him again on the forehead before leaving the room. He did not immediately fall asleep, but rolled over on his side and stared at the wall for a while. He has survived, along with most of the others. But Eldon was gone, the cook's daughter was never coming home, and Jessica would never smile at him ever again. Those losses were not acceptable, not in his kingdom, and from here onward Waldemar would do everything in his power to keep his subjects safe from all harm to the best of his abilities.

Weldon stood there and stared out over the city with an eye toward the house where everything happened that day. He heard the rustle of a skirt and turned to see Lady Rana had come out on the balcony.

"I am surprised you have not gone home to Daniella yet," Lady Rana said.

"There are still some things I have to do before I can head home," Weldon replied, "Where is your daughter?"

"I left her with the carriage," Lady Rana answered, "She promised me that she was responsible enough to bring it here and since the coachman is going to make sure it gets here, I feel it is safe to let her do so. What else did they find in the house?"

"Bodies in a room in the cellar that the demon was using as a hiding place," Weldon said, "And a room on the upper floor which was painted with all sorts of symbols."

"You are having the captain of the guard pull out the bodies, right?" Lady Rana asked.

"The ones from the cellar," Weldon answered.

"And then what?" Lady Rana asked.

There was a loud crash and then flames leapt into the air where the house was. Weldon and Lady Rana looked over. The building had quickly been engulfed in the flames. The guards were working hard to keep the sparks and heat from lighting the houses nearby on fire. Anyone else around was just watching the place burn.

"That is a good option," Lady Rana said as they continued to watch.

"Unless I am mistaken it is the best way to deal with anything that might have a magic source," Weldon said.

"As far as I know," Lady Rana said, "If it does not burn you will know when it is finished and then we will have to figure out what to do with it."

"I hope there is nothing left," Weldon said.

"We fought and won against both demons," Lady Rana said, "That is a good record."

"And what if there is a next time?" Weldon asked, "Will we be so lucky then?"

"I do not have any answers as far as next time," Lady Rana answered, "All I know is we survived this one and should be grateful for that before we worry about the future."

"Why would Lord or Lady Travers want to summon a demon?" Weldon asked.

"Do they have any children who could provide an

answer to such as question?" Lady Rana asked.

"I do not know," Weldon answered, "I have not looked it up."

"The house will continue to burn for a while," Lady Rana said, "You might want to know before they show up to find out what happened to their parent's house."

Weldon thought about that for a moment before he nodded. He headed inside and went to his office. He found the family tree for the Travers and opened it up. There was one name after Lord and Lady Travers and it was their daughter. The name seemed familiar, but it was only as he was putting the book away that he realized why. Lord and Lady Travers's daughter had married the son of Lord Laban shortly before both men stopped coming to court. As far as Weldon knew they lived at a country estate because they did not like the gossip of living at court.

Weldon sat down and took out a piece of letter paper. He composed a letter about the fire that no one was sure how it started and both Lord Travers, Lady Travers, and all the servants had been inside when it happened. He was very apologetic about the whole thing, but he did need to know what to do with the estate. When Weldon was sure he had covered everything without saying anything about what actually happened, he folded the paper up, put it into an envelope, and sealed it. He put it in the pile with the rest of the letters to go out as soon as everything was back to normal at the castle.

Then Weldon left his office and started back toward the balcony. He did not quite reach it when the cook's assistant stopped him.

"Is it true?" she asked, "His daughter is dead?"

"Unfortunately, it is true," Weldon answered, "We will have a service for everyone who died in a few days."

"Might as well start looking for a new cook as well," the cook's assistant said, "He will not be useful for anything anymore after this."

"I will take that under advisement," Weldon said, "But I cannot do anything about it for a day or two."

"Fine," the cook's assistant shrugged before heading back toward the kitchen.

Weldon continued up to the balcony. Lady Rana was still up there and watching.

"Well?" Lady Rana asked.

"They have a daughter," Weldon answered, "I wrote her a letter, which will get delivered as soon as the messenger service is running again."

"Good," Lady Rana said. Before she could say anything else, there was a loud bang from the house that went with a huge plume of smoke, which resembled a human head. Both stared in horror at it, but then it dissipated in the wind.

"I hope that was the end of whatever that was," Weldon said.

"I think it was," Lady Rana replied, "It seemed like the final word in a long-running argument."

"I hope there are no repercussions from this," Weldon said for the first time being nervous about ordering the house to be burnt.

"I think we will be fine," Lady Rana said. They both stayed out on the balcony and watched the house burn to the ground. The captain of the guard did his best to burn as much of the house as he could, which Weldon watched and felt he did a good job of. When everything was out, Weldon headed back off to find the castle steward. He needed to find out who all was dead and help with family notifications as well as organizing the funeral service.

Waldemar did not know what time it was when he woke up, but it was still dark out. He had dreamed of Jessica sitting in a place he could not see due to mist around her and she was telling him that she was in paradise where she would wait for him. When he got there, they would read books together and play games.

Getting out of bed, Waldemar lit the candle which sat near his bed for nights when he was sick and someone had to sit up with him. He tended to use it on nights when he stayed up reading, but no one had said anything to him about burning it down. Waldemar used the candle to get to his desk, where he sat down. There was plenty of paper on it, but he took out a notebook he was supposed to use for his lessons. He turned to the first page and got his quill and ink ready.

He carefully wrote at the top of the page. For Jessica, may we get to tell stories to each other in paradise. Then he moved farther down the page. In the middle, he wrote the title of the first story, which was Dalton's Button Collection. Starting the next line on the left margin, Waldemar started writing the story of Dalton the Gremlin and his button collecting.

It did not take Waldemar long to finish writing to story down as he remembered it. Then he sat for a moment. There was another story sitting in his head waiting for the quill to dip itself into the ink and reach out for the page, but his head stopped his hand. Finally, Waldemar gave in and let his hand write the story.

There were two good friends, who lived together in a palace. They were never meant to be friends as far as those around them were concerned, but that hardly stopped them. One was named Albert and was the prince of the kingdom and the other was Victoria and she worked in the castle laundry. They met up at breakfast because he would sneak in and eat with the servants before having a second breakfast with his parents in the royal dining hall. And they would meet up at the end of the day when her work day would be done and she had some time to spare.

They would go up to the top of the tower to sit and talk. They had so many things they talked about. They talked about how it was to work in the laundry, washing all the clothes people living in the castle dirtied. They talked about his lessons on politics, history, and geometry. They talked about his father's decisions and how they affected the people of the kingdom. They talked about the queen's obsession with looking young. They talked about the mischief his younger sister got into during the day. They talked about the castle steward's mismanagement of the funds given to him to run the castle. They talked about what court gossip they had heard that day. They talked about what gossip was going around the servants' quarters for that day. They talked about the weather. They talked about the predictions for the season ahead. They talked about everything in their lives.

On the evenings when Victoria could not get away, Albert sat up there and stared up at the stars. Those were the evenings he felt the most alone. He was like one of those stars up in the heavens. Sure there were plenty of stars up there, but each one had its own separate space. He was lonely and wished she could be there, but he could not ask for her to be given time off because then she would get treated differently by her fellow workers. After all, if you were the prince's friend, then you could get all kinds of special treatment for your fellow servants even if you never had such treatment yourself.

During the days, when Albert was not busy with lessons many of the daughters of the nobles at court would hang around his activities as if he would notice them and talk to them. He had tried a few times, but always found them to be infuriatingly brainless. Their goal in life was to snag a prince and be taken care of for the rest of their lives. Their life did not truly have a purpose and they had not goals in life. They also lacked opinions on anything other than what was currently fashionable and current court gossip.

When the king held dances, the girls would spend much of the time looking at Albert and batting their eyes. He danced with a different girl for each song and made sure to never dance with anyone twice, or even make much conversation with them. Anything that might show any sort of preference for a particular girl meant his mother would try to set him up with her later in the week thinking that this might be the right girl for him. He looked forward to the next night when he could spend it talking with Victoria. Victoria could not go to the dances because such things would cause trouble for everyone and Albert would never see Victoria ever again.

The trouble started on Albert's sixteenth birthday. In this particular kingdom, adulthood was considered to start at sixteen, but as a prince, Albert's life would not start until his father either died or abdicated. However, Albert's morning started off with him unable to slip into breakfast with the servants because his father met him at his bedroom door and escorted Albert down to the royal dining hall. He politely endured hugs from his mother and his grandmother, who was still alive and causing no end of trouble for the king as she was outspoken and considered crazy. His sister did not make it down for breakfast, for which Albert was grateful. No one knew what kind of trick she was going to pull next. Breakfast itself was not exciting as it was Albert's least favourite thing to eat for breakfast and it was never served to the servants.

After breakfast, instead of lessons, Albert was dragged off with his father for a morning hunt. Albert had his own falcon, but he disliked hunting with his father because the king was always giving him tips on how to hunt. None of them were any use to Albert because he had become better than his father several years ago. His father only hunted occasionally, while Albert had hunted regularly all his life. They stayed out all morning with the hunt. All that time, Albert felt like his father wanted to say something to him, but never quite found the right awkward pause to fill with it. They rode back without his father bringing the subject up.

Lunch was a quiet affair as his sister had gone to a friend's house and the king had to attend to other things. It was just him and his mother in the dining hall and she spent the entire time talking about a princess visiting from a nearby kingdom and the outrageous fashions she had brought with her. Albert did not know anything about this princess and merely nodded throughout the meal while thinking about how long it would be before he could meet up with Victoria and talk the evening away.

After lunch, Albert tried to sneak away to some place quiet, but he was caught and sent to talk to his father. When Albert arrived in the throne room, his mother was sitting on the throne beside his father on his throne. They were presenting a solid front for whatever they wanted to speak to him because they knew he was not going to agree with it. He wanted to leave before they could start, but he could not because there would be severe consequences. Instead, Albert went and bowed to his parents.

"We have a matter of profound importance we need to speak with you about," the king said. Albert waited him out because there was no point interrupting him, even though he paused as if he expected Albert to say something.

"We are concerned about the future of this kingdom," the king said, "And we feel you are not taking your part in it seriously." Another pause for Albert to wonder what his father was talking about.

"We have watched from a distance as you show no interest in any of the ladies at court," the king said, "And we feel troubled by this." Albert wondered if his father paused to torture him, or whether he even realized he was doing it.

"As a result, we have taken the matter into our own hands," he king said, "And we feel this is the right decision." Albert did not like the way this 'talk' was going.

"We received a letter from the neighbouring kingdom about their need to find a husband for their princess," the king said, "And we feel this princess would be the perfect match for you." Albert kept

his face composed in the same expressionless mask he always wore in front of his father.

"The princess arrived yesterday and will be presented to you in an hour," the king said, "And we feel that you should be dressed appropriately for the occasion."

His father went on for a little bit more about princesses marrying princes, as well as how this match was good for Albert, but Albert barely listened to him. He had no interest in marrying this princess, or any others his parents could come up with; though his father said something about the wedding being only a couple days away.

Finally, they let him leave to get prepared for the viewing. Albert went to his room, where his valet had already been warned about this event. Despite his valet already having an outfit picked out, Albert went through his closet for the outfit he wore only at funerals. He set it out and the valet, despite knowing better, dressed him in it.

The king and queen were wearing something nice for this event and would have sent Albert up to change out of the black, drab outfit he had turned up in, but there was no time. The princess arrived in a frilly pink dress with matching everything. She looked like if she was out in the flower garden, the bees might mistake her for a flower. Albert was introduced to the princess and she was introduced to him, but they spoke little and she giggled like a five-year-old at an adult tea party, which grated Albert's nerves.

The princess was also there in the dining hall for supper and seated near Albert so that they could talk. She chattered on about nothing while he developed a migraine. Only once supper was over was he able to excuse himself from her company and go met up with Victoria. She was sitting drawn into herself and staring out the window. All his worries drained away and his only concern was Victoria's troubles.

She cried as she told him that they could not meet anymore. He wanted to cry with her when she explained that her father had arranged a marriage for her with a man who worked in the castle stable. She was to be married to the horrible man in two days' time. Albert wanted to tell her that it would turn out all right, but he knew his own wedding was being planned in the same short amount of time. And as much as he would love to be the hero and save them both, he could not think of any way to do such a thing. Instead, they agreed to meet one last time the next night and went their own ways for the night.

The next morning, Albert's grandmother found him moodily staring out the window in the library as he sulked. Albert had spent the night thinking about the situation and came to the realization that he loved Victoria. He could not imagine a life without her and here they were about to be parted permanently.

"What is your issue?" his grandmother demanded next to his ear causing him to jump, "It is this silly marriage, is it not?"

"My father does not feel that it is silly," Albert replied.

"Your father has gotten fat in the head," his grandmother said, "The crown has squished his brain and that bride of his has screwed the common sense right out of him."

Albert stared at his grandmother. She was for saying whatever was on her mind, but never this insulting.

"You got a girl, do you not?" his grandmother demanded.

"She is being given to someone else," Albert replied.

"Well, then you have the perfect answer to both your problems," his grandmother said, "Run off together and get married before anyone can catch you. There is a chapel a county away that will marry anyone for the price of a marriage license. Twenty silver pieces are not much when you are a prince in need of a rescue." With that, his grandmother left him alone in the library. Albert did not have to think about it about but waited half an hour to make sure his grandmother was really gone.

Albert went back to his room, dismissed his valet for the rest of the day. This was not unusual behaviour for Albert and his valet had things to get ready for the wedding. Albert knew he had his rooms to himself until at least tomorrow morning. He packed a bag with two outfits for himself, some clothes for Victoria, and enough money to last a month. Then he hid the pack, just in case, and spent the rest of the day biding his time.

That evening, Albert took the pack with him when he went to meet Victoria in the tower. She was still sad, but happy to spend this brief time with him. For the first time, Albert admitted his feelings for Victoria. She admitted to having the same for him, but that they just made it harder for her to marry someone else. Then Albert told her his plan and she accepted immediately. They took the pack and snuck out of the castle.

The two managed to get to the chapel by breakfast time, but the pursuit was not far behind him because the king had gone to Albert's room to give him some advice on marriage before the big day and found him gone. After a search of the castle, it was determined that Albert had run away. However, Albert and Victoria arrived at the chapel before their pursuers. They paid for the license and the minister went through the ceremony with them. The king's men arrived in time to be witness to the kiss and pronouncement.

Albert and Victoria were dragged back to the king, but he could do nothing about their marriage because the church married them properly and the king had no control over the church. As soon as the princess heard, she left in a huff. Meanwhile, Albert and Victoria were able to live happily ever after.

Waldemar read it over Jessica's grave a week later to see if she liked it. He did that for each story in the book until it was filled.

THE END?

Mitchell put the book down on the table beside him. He looked out the window and realized that Thompson was late. Mitchell briefly wondered if he should send a message to inquire about the lateness, but decided against it. Thompson would arrive when he was ready.

Mitchell stood up and walked over to the box of books. He placed the one back inside and took out the next one. Going back to his chair, Mitchell made himself comfortable. He opened it up to the first page and started to read.

Aldous was glad when the guards finally removed his shackles and-

A knock came at the door interrupting Mitchell. He looked up from the book to see the butler opening the door to let Thompson inside. Mitchell stood up.

"Good afternoon," Mitchell said.

"Good afternoon," Thompson replied, "I am sorry I am late."

"It is all right," Mitchell said, "I have found other

things to keep me busy." Mitchell placed the book down on the table and moved toward the desk. Thompson followed him over while the butler closed the door on his way out. The men sat down and worked over the problem Thompson needed help with.

As Mitchell was drawing up the final papers, Thompson picked up the book from the table beside the chair.

"I do not recall this book in your collection before," Thompson said.

"I only recently found it," Mitchell did not look up from the papers as he filled in the last of the information.

"Is it any good?" Thompson asked.

"You know that if it was any good the Lord Secretary would have confiscated it by now," Mitchell said.

"He may be able to sense what most people are reading, but if he were able to do that with you, your library would be much smaller," Thompson said.

"I need your signature here," Mitchell flipped the papers around and pointed to an empty line. Thompson came back to the desk and set down the book before picking up the pen.

"And the book is fascinating," Mitchell said as he picked the book up. Thompson finished with the papers and sat back in the chair he had been sitting in before.

"Let's hear it," Thompson said. Mitchell opened the book and started reading out loud starting with the first line.

ABOUT THE AUTHOR

Heather Mantler is a lover of fairy tales and fables. Her home town is Prince George, British Columbia. Heather is always working on another story as she hopes to finish every story idea that she has ever written down. She was a nominee for the fiction category of the 2012 Prince George Regional Arts and Cultural Awards and short listed for the 2013 John Harris Fiction Awards. Her blog is heathersdomain.wordpress.com. Heather encourages her readers to post reviews on Good Reads and Amazon.